— THE —
DRUMAULIAN CHRONICLES

A Hero's Awakening

J. TERRIGAN ROARK

NEWMAN SPRINGS PUBLISHING
320 Broad Street
Red Bank, NJ 07701

First originally published by Newman Springs Publishing 2023

ISBN 978-1-63881-488-7 (Paperback)
ISBN 978-1-63881-489-4 (Digital)

Printed in the United States of America

For my brother and family, thank you for helping me.

In loving memory of Edna Roark.

ACKNOWLEDGEMENTS

A big shout out to my friends Ethan, Austin, Matt, and Kyle. Their friendships helped me inspire characters and materials I couldn't have went without. Thanks a lot you guys are the best friends a man could ask for!

CHAPTER 1

AN AWAKENING

A hooded figure glides smoothly along the forest floor without a sound. It comes to a clearing in the forest and stops, then it removes the hood to reveal a young man with a strong square chin and full cheeks. His face was battle-hardened, yet his eyes, matching the blue haze of the suns, were still filled with the light of hope. He peered about cautiously to make sure he was alone. After a few moments, he removed his bow and quiver and propped them up on a mossy boulder as he looked around enjoying the beauty before him. He placed one hand against the moss and inhaled thinking to himself, *Ah...this is perfect.* His eyes danced with light as he took off his cloak to reveal rippled, scarred arms that showed years of combat, despite his youth. Rolling his shoulders in relief from the weight of the cloak, he spread across the boulder and sat back to rest his legs. He sighed and spoke softly as if to the forest itself, "I love this place."

He looked up to the sky and watched as a great eagle scouted the treetops for a quick kill. Its massive wings were able to carry a large deer away. Lifting his hand, he tracked the eagle's path, then his eyes widened as its wings folded, and it dove straight for him. Rolling quickly to the side, he reached for his bow as he sprang to his feet and sprinted for the tree line. Turning to see the eagle's talons just a few feet away, he fired his bow in a final act of desperation. Watching as the arrow left the guidance of his finger, he raised his hand up, palm first, to shield himself from the oncoming attack. He frowned in confusion as time seemed to slow and nearly halt. He cautiously moved forward and noticed its feathers were beautiful shades of yellow, red, and blue, with a green plume on its head. Eyes wide with wonder, he walked to view the eagle from behind. As soon as he stopped moving and dropped his hand, he gasped in shock as he watched the event unfold before his eyes: time resumed normal speed, and the arrow was buried into the eagle's chest, killing it instantly.

He stood confused at what he had just done. *Am I a demon?* he thought to himself. *No, not a demon. I can't be, I can enter the holy temples, and Quinn said demons can't. Not that I've ever met one,* he thought to himself. He paced to and fro, staring at his hands then stopping to look at the eagle. A twig snapped, and he notched another arrow, drawing his bow. "Who's there?" he shouted, aiming directly where he heard the sound. A fox jumped out of the trees and yelped then cackled as it ran away. "Just a fox," he muttered as he sighed and lowered his guard.

He gathered his belongings quickly then turned to the eagle and cracked a smile. "It's a shame I had to kill you, you were a pretty bird. I need to find a way to save those feathers," he added, looking at its wings. *Well, I can't just let him go to waste,* he thought to himself. He rummaged through his pack and pulled out a small rope then tied it to the eagle's feet. He rummaged in his pack some more and shoved half of his body inside. "Damn magic pack! It comes in handy, but Catia puts way too much of her stuff in it when I'm at her place!" His muffled complaints were the only sound to be heard minus a slight echo of hoof beats.

"Finally, holy shit!" he groaned as he stepped on the bottom of his pack then proceeded to pull himself out of it. He strained with all his might, but he could not free himself. "Oh gods, not again!" he moaned. He raised up then started running as fast as he could in a straight line until he hit a nearby tree and bounced off. "Found one," he whimpered as he struggled to his feet. He approached the tree slowly until the entire pack was against it. "Okay, gimmie a low branch here, Itrius man, c'mon," he puffed as he walked around the tree. As fate would have it, the tree had a low broken branch that snagged the pack and freed Rinn of his bonds. He came out with a large tarp and a longer rope. He checked his surroundings and located his kill. He trotted over and spread the tarp out on the ground next to the corpse. He walked to the far side of the eagle and started to roll it onto the tarp when it suddenly bit him on the arm. Out of instinct, he pulled a knife and stabbed it in the eye. "Perhaps he wasn't all the way dead," he added, looking to his arm, which was halfway covered with his own blood.

Should be fine, he thought to himself as he resumed his task. He rolled it up in the tarp then used the longer rope to tie the tarp closed. He then moved to the eagle's feet. He tugged the rope, testing the weight with one arm, straining at the weight of the beast. He pulled a bit harder and moved the corpse: he threw the rope over his shoulder, adjusted his grip, pulled with all his strength, and then began to haul the eagle through the woods.

"Maybe someone will help me get you to the market." He chuckled out loud as he began to strain out a song.

> And so I flew away for breakfast and little did I know,
> a small man would end my life with his bow!
> Oh why, oh why didn't I fly to the river?
> Instead I got an arrow from a quiver!
> What might could bring me to an end?
> Why me! Rinn! The mightiest of men!

He dragged the corpse further through the woods, only stopping for a sip of water every hour or so. Rinn had been pulling till midnoon sun was high in the sky when he came across the old road. He stopped and rolled the eagle's body down the bank, causing one of its feathers to come loose. He stooped over and retrieved the feather and paused long enough to braid it into his wavy black hair. Rinn looked to the sky to see that the cool of the day was coming to a swift end, the second sun was on the horizon. He looked either direction, up and down the road, in hopes of a wagon, a farmer with a steer, any form of transportation to the agora, hoping he could get there quickly. He glanced toward the rising blue sun with apprehension, knowing he would need to get to the agora before the swarm of flies that rose with the blue haze set in.

He shrugged hopelessly and continued to drag the corpse to the agora. *I can't be too far off now. One hour at the most,* he thought. "You better be worth it, you fat bastard," he said aloud to himself. He kept going when suddenly he began to hear the faint creaking and squeaking of a wagon approaching him from behind. Rinn stopped and waited for the stranger, then turned to greet them with a smile in hopes they were someone he knew.

The stranger pulled the reigns back. "Whoa, whoa!" he called out. Then he hopped off the wagon and stared at Rinn in awe. His snow-white bushy beard and his brows hid his eyes, giving off the impression of an old man. "Did you do this, son?" He let out in a voice that made him sound as if he was gargling peanut butter.

"Yes, sir, I did," he exclaimed with pride.

"How?" the man asked as he folded his arms in disbelief.

"Well, I shot him, then I stabbed him in the eye," Rinn responded plainly as he ran his fingers through his long, wavy hair. "I'm not sure how else to put it really"—he turned to the stranger—"do you think you could be generous enough to haul me and him to the agora?" he queried, holding out his pockets, revealing he had no money.

"Young man, it's not in my nature to give out to strangers," he said in a stern tone.

"I see," Rinn returned, lowering his head. As he turned, crestfallen, to the eagle and picked up his rope, he said, "I'll let you be on your way then." He grunted as he resumed dragging the eagle.

The old man put a hand on his shoulder to stop him. "Now, wait just a minute, young man. What's your name?" the old man asked with a smile.

"My name is Rinn," he answered, full of pride.

"Well, young man"—he stuck out his hand—"I'm Ajon. Pleased to meet you," he claimed as he and Rinn shook hands. With his smile still firmly in place and his eyes twinkling, he added, "Well, since we ain't strangers no more, let's load up the big bastard!"

"All right!" Rinn exclaimed with joy. The two of them grabbed it by its feet and lifted it up into the wagon with surprising ease. Rinn looked at his new acquaintance and grinned. "So to the agora then, eh?"

"Aye, son. Let's go, times a wastin'," he called as he hopped on the wagon with surprising agility for his age.

"Right then," Rinn agreed as he hopped up on the back of the wagon and stepped over into the seat. "So, Ajon," he began, "might I ask where you're from? I know everyone in this area, and I've yet to see or hear of you as far as I can remember."

"Hold on just a minute there, you two," a hooded man said as he stepped out of the tree line.

"And who might you be, good sir?" Ajon queried, raising a bushy brow in suspicion.

"I'm nobody special. I'm only worth fifteen gold pieces," the man replied, brandishing a pair of daggers.

"Your name?" Rinn inquired from under his hood.

"Marco the Butcher at your service," he replied with a bow.

"A bounty!" Rinn exclaimed as he shed his cloak. "C'mon then!" he added drawing his sword.

"Just who do you think you are, kid?" Marco asked as the rest of his men revealed themselves.

"Rinn, captain of the Dogs of War at your service," he replied with a mischievous grin.

"It's him!" one of the men shouted in fear.

"Steady lads! He can't take us all at once!" Marco ordered but turned to discover his men had already fled. "Damn pussies," he scoffed.

"You shouldn't take your eyes off me," Rinn said menacingly as he pressed his sword against Marco's throat.

"You're as fast as lightning kid," Marco responded, dropping his daggers.

"That's just because you weren't looking," Rinn said as he put a fan in Marco's hands and tied them up with a spare rope from his pack.

"Why the fan?" Marco asked, looking at it in confusion.

"Keep the flies off my eagle or I'll kill you," Rinn replied as he tied Marco's legs together and threw him in the back of the wagon.

"All right, just don't kill me," Marco said, holding up the fan.

"That depends on how you treat that fan. Someone very special gave that to me," Rinn replied, flicking his sword out of its sheath with his thumb, just barely revealing the blade. Marco's eyes widened, and he gave a nervous smile and started fanning desperately.

"Now then, to the agora?" Ajon queried, looking over to Rinn.

"Yeah, let's go. Those other guys are long gone," Rinn said as he climbed onto the wagon.

"Never seen a dozen men run from a name before," Ajon said with a smile.

"Tends to happen when a hundred men armed to the teeth can't even touch a boy using his fists," Marco puffed as he fanned the eagle's corpse.

"A hundred is about fifty short, thank you very much. Also, none of that would've happened if your men hadn't kidnapped my student for ransom money!" Rinn snapped, pointing his hand at Marco.

"Well, what happened in the past doesn't matter," Marco responded, lowering his head in shame.

"There's Constable O'Malley!" Rinn shouted as he spied a burly, red-headed man wearing a pair of thick leather overalls with a thick mustache. "Constable!" he shouted as he hopped off the still moving wagon.

"Oh, my stars! Good after-noon, laddie! What brings you into town today?" Constable O'Malley queried with a big smile.

"I snagged Marco the Butcher on my way in. Have you got enough gold to pay the bounty for him on you?" Rinn queried as he flipped Marco upside down over the side of the wagon.

"Aye sure I do, lad. Hold on just a minute," O'Malley replied as he fumbled around in his pouch and pulled out fifteen gold pieces and handed them to Rinn.

"Thank you, kindly sir. He's all yours," Rinn said, pointing at Marco.

"No problem, lad. Pleasure doin' business with ya," O'Malley replied as he pulled a set of shackles out of his pouch. He shackled

Marco then untied the ropes to be sure that he couldn't run away. Suddenly, Marco threw the fan as far as he could into the woods.

"Hey, you little petty shit! That was a gift from someone very special!" Rinn snapped as he threw a punch that connected with Marco's jaw, knocking him cold. "Dammit, now I have to go get it," he puffed. "Sorry, constable," he said as he wandered into the woods.

"Don't worry about it, he's no trouble to drag to the jail," O'Malley replied. "It's been a while, Aesiri. How've you been?" he queried, looking to Ajon.

"Quiet now, the boy doesn't know anything. I've been grand, though thanks for asking," Ajon replied. "And how about you, General O'Malley?" he queried, raising a brow and revealing how his eyes looked like burning coals.

"Oho! How nostalgic! I haven't been known by that title in a couple decades now. I've been grand as well. I married Lielu, and we had a strong boy named Matthaeus. He grew up with young Rinn and leads the Mercenary Guild in town," O'Malley replied, rubbing his mustache.

"I'm sure he's about to figure it all out. I came here to find Quinn," Ajon explained.

"Well, I better be outta here before he gets back," O'Malley said as he grabbed the chains around Marco's feet and started dragging him down the road "No need to worry about me walking too far. My horse is just down the road, I pissed him off again. I'm just going to tie him to this tree up ahead," he added as he started to haul the criminal into the distance.

"What'd you say to him this time?" Ajon inquired with a grin.

"I called him a dafty bastard," O'Malley sighed as he continued walking. Ajon simply sat in silence and waited for Rinn to return. He leaned back and pulled his hat over his eyes as if he were about to take a nap when Rinn came stumbling out of the woods, holding the fan in his hand.

"Gods know what she'd do to me if I lost another gift," Rinn puffed as he climbed back onto the wagon. "I believe I was asking you where you're from before all this happened," he added with a sigh.

"You're not one who forgets things, are you?" Ajon queried, peeking from under his hat.

"Nope, so out with it. Where do you come from?" Rinn queried back, clearly suspicious of his new acquaintance.

"You're also a little rude, aren't you?" Ajon asked with a blank expression. Rinn just stared back with a blank expression and waited in silence for a few moments.

"Well, are you gonna tell me or what?" Rin shouted, frowning.

"I don't really have a home anymore. Not since I lost my huntin' partner," Ajon explained as he whipped the reigns and started toward the town. "I've been on the road for quite some time now—basically, ever since I was a boy. But now I've been trying to get back into the huntin' business, y'know." He looked at Rinn and smiled. "And what about you, lad? Where do you hail from?" he queried.

"Well, I'm not sure where I'm from really. My mother and father died when I was too young to remember their names, and I was raised by Quinn, a friend of my father's. He was the one who taught me to shoot a bow and how to wield a sword. He is my father, as far as I'm concerned," he added as he looked up to the sky and sighed. Suddenly, a putrid smell wafted from behind him. "Is it just me, or do I smell something?" he queried, looking over his shoulder.

"Your nose must be like a hound's, son. I can't smell anything besides the horses' asses," Ajon chuckled amiably as he cracked the reigns and encouraged his horses to a quicker gate. *So he can smell demons,* he thought to himself.

"Did you just say something about demons?" Rinn asked, looking over suspiciously.

"Why would I say something about demons?" Ajon responded with a blank expression.

"Fair point," Rinn replied, keeping a constant eye on him. They continued onward, chatting and laughing together until they saw the town in the distance.

"Is that your agora there?" Ajon inquired as he slowed the wagon as they made their way to the edge of town. "We'll be runnin' out of time soon ya know, son. Let's sell this beastly boy," he muttered under his breath as he started toward the agora. Ajon sighed and frowned as the wagon swayed.

"What's wrong, friend? Somethin' on your mind?" Rinn asked, looking at him with concern.

"Ah, it's nothin', lad. I need not worry you about it," Ajon returned as his smile returned to his face. "What's your livin', son?" he asked, effectively changing the subject.

"My skills with a bow and blade got me on as a guard for Lord Theon. I'm on my way there now actually. I'm the personal guard of his daughter, Catia, although previously I was head captain of the mercenary guild. No paperwork, and I still got to tell people what to do. But the new job has certain benefits that I couldn't pass up," Rinn smiled with pride and held his hand on his chest.

"Ah! So this Catia, is she um...beautiful?" Ajon asked with a laugh.

"Yes, very beautiful. Her hair is a blaze of fire, her skin as fair as the first moon, and her eyes rival the eastern sea. I can't understand anything they say in that country though," Rinn answered as he looked up to the sky and sighed. "It's been nearly seventeen years since I first laid eyes on her." He pulled a small locket out of his shirt. "Gods above know how much I love her. But her father could never know. He'd kill me for even thinking of her in that way." He tucked the locket away under his shirt.

"Ah, but forbidden fruit is always the sweetest," Ajon claimed as he glanced at Rinn and stroked his beard. "Son, I'm wondering somethin'," he said as he blew through his beard.

"Yes?" Rinn raised a brow and grinned.

"You seem like the average fella, but tell me somethin'. How'd you dodge that eagle when he dove for you?" he inquired as he glanced Rinn with a raised brow.

"How long have you been following me?" Rinn asked suspiciously. He watched him carefully in anticipation of an attack.

"Easy son, I'm not the one out to hurt you, I swear on my word as a man. It's your power that'll get you killed," Ajon returned as he waited for Rinn's reaction, but none came. He looked him over, studying his behavior. He knew Rinn wouldn't harm him unless he made him. Ajon's years of hunting experience gave him the ability to read peoples' emotions, even when they didn't understand them themselves.

"You were the sound I heard," Rinn lowered his guard, still watching Ajon.

"No, son, I was behind you the whole way. You do realize that you're very loud in the woods? Talkin' to yourself like that is a dead giveaway. You should be quieter," Ajon folded his arms.

Rinn sat in silence for a moment and looked at him "What did you hunt, Ajon?"

"I hunted whatever I was paid to hunt. I started with beasts like the one you have here now, lad. But I eventually began to hunt down men. I hunted men for the remainder of my career, and I enjoyed it. I was paid by bad men to kill worse men, and they all got what they deserved in the end." His eyes grew hollow under his brow as he looked ahead.

Rinn looked at Ajon, and his eyes widened as he realized he was looking at the most famed killer his world had ever known, an immortal spirit of vengeance. "Your name isn't Ajon, is it?"

"No, I'm afraid not, son. My name is Soko. Soko the Soulless, some called me. But just call me Ko," he replied with a smile.

"I've heard your legend," Rinn drew his sword, and in the blink of an eye, it was at Soko's throat. "Give me good reason why it shouldn't end here and now." He pressed the edge of his blade against Soko's beard.

"If I wanted you dead, you would be. Now relax and get your toothpick off my beard." He looked at Rinn and gestured at his entirety. "I can teach you how to move like that whenever you want. After all, I've been nothing but kind to you so far. Who's to say my legend is true?"

"What're you getting at?" Rinn eased the sword off his throat but kept it pointed at him. "What makes you think you can teach me how to use it?"

"Believe me or not, you're not the first person I've known that can do that, move like lightning. I knew a great man that could do that. But sadly, he died long ago. I've been looking for you ever since." He put his finger on the tip of the sword and guided it away slowly. "Heh. Now, what's your answer?" he looked at Rinn with eyes of coal that could paralyze a man in his boots.

Rinn looked back with eyes of ice. *Those eyes, I've never seen anything like them,* Rinn thought to himself. He cleared his throat. "I'll give you an answer in the morning. Until then, get me to the market. I have to sell this eagle or supplies will be short on my next assignment," he said sternly.

"Right, let's go then." Two clicks and they were moving again. The two of them traveled along the simple street in search of a butcher. They hopped off the wagon and ventured into the market. While Soko watered his horses, Rinn looked about for a merchant or butcher to trade with. He disappeared into the crowd and came back in the company of a small, husky man in a bloody apron.

"Hot damn, that's a big boy!" the butcher let out in a booming voice.

"What would you give for him?" Rinn asked with a smile.

"What would you take for him, lad?" he inquired as he placed an arm on his belly.

"A few pounds of dried meat, a bag of sweets, a keg of ale, and water. Lots of water. About three or four five-gallon sacks." Rinn looked at the butcher as he stood with an arm propped up on his gut and another rubbing his face. He reached down to lift up a leg to test the weight and turned to Rinn.

"Well, I don't have all those supplies. How's two bags of silver sound?" he looked at Rinn, still rubbing his face.

"Throw in the dried meats, and we've got a deal," he looked at the butcher, sure of himself, and folded his arms.

"I dunno if I can make that happen, laddie." He scratched his head and blew through his thick mustache.

Soko stepped in and mumbled something inaudible into the butcher's ear. Then he patted his shoulder and the butcher left, disappearing into the crowd.

"Where is he going? What did you just do?" Rinn scowled at him and waited for an answer.

"Don't get all pissy with me son, he'll be back. With three bags of silver, four pounds of dried beef, and one pound of fresh pork for tonight," retorted Soko. Rinn stood in confusion and stared at him. "What? Do you think you're the only one with a few tricks?"

Rinn remained silent and shrugged it off, but he started getting wary of his companion. *How can I trust him? He's a cold-blooded monster. Quinn told me he once killed everyone in a whole town to get one man. I don't trust him. But I have to know what he knows. Maybe I can use him,* he thought to himself. "How did you do that? What did you do to make him do what you wanted?" he queried to Soko under his breath.

"That, son, is a skill I picked up from my huntin' partner. I can simply bend someone's mind enough to make them think what I tell them to do is a good idea. Even if it's to take a life or end their own," Soko replied.

"That's dark magic! You're a devil! You're no man at all!" Rinn reached for his sword, but before he could blink, Soko's coal-black eyes were an inch away.

"Let's not do anything hasty, shall we?" Soko's eyes seemed to burn with small embers. He stared deep into Rinn's soul. *I've only seen one man with eyes like this. Could he be?* he thought to himself.

Rinn stood sternly. He studied every detail he could. *If I make the wrong move now, one of us will die.* Rinn let loose of his sword "We're going somewhere when the butcher gets back. There's someone you're going to meet. It won't be long. And no, you don't have a choice in the matter."

"What makes you think you can tell me what to do?" Soko snapped.

"You're a wanted killer, and I'll turn you into my Lord if you don't." Rinn looked at him, blatantly raising a brow as he plucked some wing and tail feathers from the eagle.

"Point taken," he turned and pointed. "Your friend is back," he added snappishly.

"Here's the silver and the meat. Have a safe trip," the butcher rolled the eagle onto his cart and disappeared into the crowd.

"Thank you, sir." Rinn turned to Soko and looked at him in shock. "What kind of dark sorcery do you have power over? What dark magic controls a man's mind?"

"It's not magic. It's just a manipulation skill" He turned and began to load all the goods onto the wagon. "Now, seeing tha' ya don't have any sweets for your sweetie, why don't we go pick some up and some of that ale you were speaking of?" He raised his bushy brows and looked at Rinn.

"Ale? Why get that when we can get a couple of kegs of Old Greyman's mead? It's stronger and honestly better tasting too." He looked at Soko and motioned him to follow. "This way, I'm getting the sweets and cheese first." They rode a bit further into town, then Rinn started thinking, *He's acting like a normal man. But what kind of man has eyes like that? It's almost demonic in nature.* The two of them ventured through the market, picking out treats and such for the journey to the palace. Neither one of them spoke a word, only smiled and nodded at the friendly shop keepers. As they made their way back to the wagon, Rinn turned to Soko. "Where did you get eyes like that?" he queried.

"I could ask the same of you. A solid blue eye isn't exactly commonplace." Soko grunted as he hopped into the wagon, then they pulled away and started toward Greyman's place.

"Mine come from my father," Rinn replied plainly.

"Of course they do," Soko replied dryly. "I got poison spit into my eyes as a child. I don't remember much of anything beyond that. My vision is fine, but I suppose these eyes helped me in my work," Soko added as he turned away from Rinn. "Now, if you'll excuse me, I'd like to nap for a while," he added as he pulled his hat over his eyes.

"Right then, I'll return with the mead shortly," Rinn pulled his hood over and walked through Greyman's like a ghost. His cloak hid everything but his chin as he ventured through in search of Greyman when he finally found him having a drink with another old man laughing away at an unknown subject. Greyman was a short, round old man with wild white hair and eyes to match. His beard hid most of his face, giving him the look of a wild man. He had a loud cackle for a laugh and didn't care for anything but strong whiskey. Rinn placed a hand on his shoulder. "Hello there, ya old drunk." Rinn chuckled. "May I sit, Greyman?"

"Of course, ya lil' bastard!" he cackled out and drank some more. "What can I do ya for?" Greyman queried.

"I was wondering if I could pick up some mead. Lord Theon is giving me another assignment, and some spirits are in order," he replied.

"Help yourself, boy. I'll take about twenty silver pieces and let you have about three kegs. One on the house there, my boy," he said, motioning for Rinn to leave, then he turned back to his conversation.

Rinn laid the silver out on the table then continued to the bar and took the three kegs out to the wagon. He loaded them up while Soko rolled in his sleep, so Rinn drove the wagon out of town to Quinn's. He ventured through the rolling fields and looked about the golden grass with no worries. *This place will forever be my home. It's always so peaceful here. I wonder if Catia has changed in these short months.* He closed his eyes and imagined her beautiful face, fiery red hair, cheeks as pink as the third moon, and eyes as if they had the whole universe inside of them. *So beautiful.* He smiled and held his locket gently. *I hope this assignment is the longest one yet.*

"Hey, dream boy!" Rinn jumped out of his skin and scowled at Quinn as he cackled and rolled in the back of the wagon. "You, you know it's funny!" he said, still rolling in laughter.

"How long have you been there anyway?" Rinn looked at Quinn with confusion.

"Oh, I hopped in the back when you left town. Who's this guy?" he said, lifting Soko's hat off his face "Oh, What's Ko-Ko doing here?"

"Ko-Ko? You know each other?" Rinn said in shock.

"Well duh, Rinn, I was his hunting partner once," Quinn said blankly.

"*What the fuck is going on here, Quinn?*" Rinn's shout woke Soko, and he rose from his sleep only to smack heads with Quinn, then he fell off the wagon with a groan.

"Who's yelling about what now? What the bloody fuck am I doing down in the road for?" Soko staggered back up to the wagon, looking like he'd been to the bottom of a barrel.

"Why the hurry, son?" Quinn hopped up to the front and looked at Rinn with a sarcastic smile.

"Who the fuck knocked me off *my* wagon?" Soko babbled out.

"You did it yourself, Ko-Ko. I was just the head you smacked," Quinn said in his finest sarcasm. "And I think you owe me an apology," he added folding his arms.

"Sorry. Wait just a fuckin' minute now. Ko-Ko? Who the fuck? *You bastard!*" Soko tackled Quinn off the wagon, and they rolled off the road into the woods. Meanwhile, Rinn halted the wagon, shaking his head. All he could hear was a barrage of profanity and twigs snapping, then Quinn crawled up to the road still in a roar of laughter.

"Lighten up, Ko-Ko, it's all good now," Quinn pleaded as he turned but was met by Soko's fist across his nose. "Gah, fuck why'd you go off and do that for, ya grumpy old troll?"

"I am not a fuckin' troll," Soko said, pointing at Quinn.

"Well, you sure do act like one!" Quinn groaned out.

Rinn sat silent and watched the two of them yell back and forth and wondered how they could have ever been friends. He wondered why he had been lied to by the man who raised him since he could remember, and he became furious with Quinn.

CHAPTER 2

THE BEGINNING

Rinn sat in silence under his hood, waiting for an answer from someone. "Be quiet," he said calmly.

"Shit, he's mad," Quinn mumbled as he suddenly stopped laughing.

"Explain," Rinn said, lowering his head and hiding the rest of his face under his hood.

"Are you sure? It's a *really* long story." Quinn asked, nervously rubbing the back of his head.

"Now. You first, Quinn." Rinn gripped the reins in his fists.

"But he just broke my nose! I can't have five minutes to clean up first?" Quinn said through his nose, still wiping the blood away.

"Fine, you have five minutes. Go clean yourself up so we can get to Lord Theon's."

Quinn headed to the stream in the forest while Soko and Rinn sat in silence. Rinn began to think to himself, *How could they be so secretive? I mentioned Quinn to Soko earlier, and he never batted an eye. Does he mean to kill us both? No, that's not it. I'd already be dead if that was the situation.*

"Soko?" Rinn asked calmly.

"Yes, friend?" Soko looked at Rinn with a smile when suddenly Rinn put his fist through Soko's face, busting his nose and mouth in a bloody mess and causing Soko to fall off the wagon. "Gah, you little fucking arse! Why'd you do that for?" he asked as he climbed back on the wagon.

"That's what you get for breaking Quinn's nose," Rinn said calmly.

"Still, though, why my nose? Couldn't it have been a jab to the ribs or something? Gods, this fucking hurts!" Soko said from behind his hands.

"Because that's fair," Rinn said as he twisted the reigns in his hands. "Does it not seem fair enough?" He sat in silence while Soko took a sullied rag out of his shirt to clean off his bloody face.

"Haha! That's what you get, you shithead!" Quinn spat out as he came to the road. "Now what in particular was I supposed to explain?" he looked at Rinn, waiting for an answer.

"How do you two know each other?" he said patiently.

"First off, what I did was keep you safe by order of the king. Secondly, I killed a lot of people to do so, and you should be a little more appreciative o. We hunted together, and he was my teacher before the world went tits up. I'm sure you know his real name. I hope this doesn't change how you feel about me, Rinn. Also, like I said, we killed many people together, but we were in our right to do so given they were trying to kill you, your mom, and your dad." Quinn sighed. "I hope you can understand." he looked down at the ground and shook his head.

"Who are *they*?" Rinn interrupted.

"Well, *they* rule this country now," Quinn replied, still hanging his head.

"Why would the Satrisia Empire want my parents' lives? They brought peace to the world," Rinn asked in confusion.

"That's what they told everyone who survived the invasion, which was only a handful of people old enough to remember. The Satrisia Empire isn't good. They came here from the underworld, they look and speak just like us, but every last one of them are evil to the core. They'll do whatever they can to gain power over the people of this world. You and your parents were the last defense by the end of it all. I'll tell you everything in due time," Quinn replied calmly.

"He did the thing," Soko said, holding his nose.

"He did the thing? The fast thing?" Quinn asked in shock.

"Yeah, that one," Soko replied as he blew blood out his nose.

"Well, you should know that you're not a normal man, Rinn. You're one of the last of Drumaul's warrior race, the Drumaulians." Quinn looked at him solemnly.

"What is that? Am I cursed by the god of war?" Rinn said, staring at his hands.

"No, you are blessed with his power to keep the peace of this world intact. The Satrisia Empire wants you dead because you and those like you are the only ones who can withstand their power," Quinn replied.

"How did they kill my mother and father? I want to know how they were defeated." Rinn looked away from Quinn and closed his eyes.

"They used a dark power from our world known as the Satrium Stone and combined it with their own dark power to defeat your father. Your mother went into a rage and almost won, but she fell as well. Their final order to me was to disappear with you, Rinn, so I had to leave them behind." Quinn hung his head between his knees.

"They had a warrior's death?" Rinn asked quietly.

"One can only hope, Rinn. I'm sorry, I couldn't see their final moments," Quinn placed a hand on Rinn's shoulder.

"You said I wasn't human. I'm something else. What does that mean?" Rinn inquired.

"When the gods created this world as a gift to their father, they created us as well. You remember learning from the nuns at the church, don't you?" Quinn replied.

"Yes, but there was only man, no others were made besides the animals," Rinn answered, crossing his eyes and watching a butterfly that had landed on his nose.

"That's part of the emperor covering his tracks. Originally, there were ten thousand of the Drumaulians, and they were Drumal's favorite creation. He blessed them with godly power to satisfy himself on watching them wage war in his name. You are descended from these people, Rinn. You could have all the power to save this world from the empire and restore the peace to the world." Quinn ruffled

Rinn's hair and smiled. "I know it's a lot to take in, but try not to freak out about it, okay?"

"But there is no war to fight, Quinn. What are you talking about?" Rinn looked up to Quinn, waiting for an answer.

"The so-called peace we have thanks to the empire is a lie. The people live in fear for their lives everywhere but here, that's why you grew up in this land. The people here live too simply and are too stubborn to be corrupted by the greed of the empire. But everywhere else the nobles take the commoners to the capitol where they're tortured to death or worse. We're lucky enough to have a Lord whose line started well before the great war. So naturally, he doesn't have anything to do with the capitol." Quinn paused and looked to the forest. "We have to be going now. It isn't wise for us to finish this talk with unwanted listeners," he added as he sat down in the back of the wagon facing the rear.

"I understand. Let's go then." Rinn cracked the reigns and they were moving. Soko was still wiping blood off his face, and Rinn looked at him. "I didn't mean to hit you so hard, I'm sorry." He pulled a rag out of his pouch and soaked it with water from a leather sack, then gave it to Soko.

"It's fine, I earned it. You hit harder than you look by the way. I bet that's why you've been so good at fighting," Soko replied as he finished wiping the blood away.

"Thanks. Would you like a drink?" inquired Rinn as he held a stone cup.

"Aye, I would," Soko took the cup and Rinn popped the cork on a keg of mead and poured it full, then he put the cork back on. "Why cork it after just one?"

"Because we've not made it to Theon's yet," Rinn said plainly.

Soko sipped the mead and swashed it around and gulped. "My, that's mighty fine stuff."

"Told you it was good." Rinn cracked the reigns and brought the horses to a trot. As the trio made their way to Theon's palace, Quinn noticed someone following in the trees off the road. They were keeping pace with the horses but couldn't hide, so he pretended to be asleep while he watched them.

"Pick up the pace," Quinn said under his breath.

"You got it." Rinn knew something was going on, and he brought the horses to a gallop. He wasn't sure what it was yet, but he didn't question Quinn on these matters. Meanwhile, Quinn was watching their mysterious follower maintain the pace of the horses.

"There is someone running us down!" Quinn shouted to Rinn in shock.

"That's not possible. The horses are galloping, they'd have to have a horse!" Rinn shouted as a man-shaped figure jumped into the road and started gaining on them. It was running them down, and there wasn't anywhere for them to go. Rinn gave the reigns to Soko as he drew his bow. He fired an arrow straight at the figure's head, but it dodged, and the arrow cut its face, causing a black flame to erupt out of the wound while its hood and clothing remained unburnt. "What the hell is this guy?" Rinn looked at Quinn and Soko for an answer, and they both shrugged and kept looking ahead. Frustrated, Rinn fired another arrow and hit the figure in the head. It dropped to its knees and exploded in a huge blast of black flame.

"That was...different," Quinn added, confused.

"I've never seen or heard of people exploding when they die. And I've killed a lot of people. Hell, those demons don't even explode," Soko muttered.

"Well, I don't think it was a human. I think it was something from that demonic realm or maybe something they created," Rinn added as he took his seat.

"You're probably right on that one, lad," Soko said into his cup.

"Why were we being followed? There's no way anyone that's not from around here could've seen. I was alone, and I don't even know how I did it," Rinn mumbled to Quinn.

"The gods intervened and saved you, Rinn, but there's no guarantee you were alone. Soko was watching you after all," Quinn said under his breath.

"I was watching you. Who knows, anyone else could've been watching me watch you," Soko said with his mouth full of mead. He swashed it around and swallowed. "You reckon they were just after me? I've been traveling on this wagon with the same two horses for quite some time now, and maybe I got sloppy a time or two and someone recognized me." He looked at his companions with dried blood in his beard, and they both laughed at him. "What's so funny about that? This is serious business, y'know!"

"It's your bloodied beard Ko-Ko! You should really wash that out." Quinn chuckled and grabbed Soko by the nose. "Does this hurt or cause you any discomfort?"

"Gods, let go! Let go! Of course it fucking hurts, ya daft bastard!" Soko squalled in pain, and Quinn released him.

"I was only curious to see if it had healed yet," Quinn said innocently.

"Will you two stop for ten minutes! Gods, you're both a headache," snapped Rinn.

"Fine," spat Quinn. The three of them traveled in silence as they made their way to the palace.

The golden fields and rolling hills no longer felt peaceful to Rinn. He kept his guard up on the off chance they had another pursuer. *What was that thing? It had to be a demon, but where did it even come from? There could be more out there watching,* Rinn thought to himself. *What if she's safer without me?* Rinn's heart grew heavy because he knew that he was right. He had to tell Theon everything that had happened.

"When will we get there anyway?" Soko babbled out.

"No more than another hour at the most. Why do you ask?" Rinn inquired with suspicion.

"Because we need to figure out what we're gonna do when we get there. You were the only one summoned, and you'll be showing up with two extra men," Soko said from under his hat.

"Well, you two just drop me off by the palace and stay close but out of sight. I have to tell Theon about what's happened." Rinn lowered his head and sighed.

"You should leave the eagle out of it," Quinn added as he took a bite of jerky.

"Right. I understand." Rinn knew he had to keep his power from Theon on the off chance he was on the empire's side. As far as Rinn knew, Theon was a kind and fair ruler to his people, and he'd never given a reason to believe otherwise. *Well, this is just the grandest thing. I have to keep an uncontrollable power under wraps and bring Catia gods know where at the same time,* he thought to himself as he looked over to Quinn, who was staring at the sky. "Quinn what are we going to do about Catia?"

"What do you mean?" he asked, still gnawing on his piece of jerky.

"I mean, how are we going to keep her unaware that something is going on with you two around? It's not like we have any type of plan or anything," Rinn added as he continued to look for anything suspicious.

"Do we really need a plan? I mean, I guess Soko and I could just follow you two lovebirds," Quinn remarked carelessly.

"We are not lovebirds!" Rinn's face turned crimson, and he pulled his hood over his head.

"Well, your face says otherwise," Quinn said, laughing.

"Aye laddie, your face is as red as a crimloch's hide!" Soko cackled, smacking his thigh

"I didn't know he'd be this easy to mess with," Quinn said mischievously as he turned toward Soko with a grin.

"What're you—?" Soko was cut off when Quinn silently shushed him and started to sneak over to Rinn's side of the wagon without a sound. Soko watched with an impish grin under his beard as Quinn crept directly behind Rinn.

"Look, there's Catia!" he said, pointing ahead.

"Where?" Rinn jumped out of his skin and scanned the whole area while Soko and Quinn rolled in laughter. "That's not even a little bit funny. You two act like children." Rinn scowled at the two of them as they continued jeering him.

"Maybe we wouldn't if you weren't rattled so easily. But maybe we would anyway, so what's it matter?" Quinn said as he was pouring himself a cup of mead.

"He's right, you know. You are rattled pretty easy," Soko added as he handed his cup to Quinn.

"No, I'm not! I don't get excited over anything," snapped Rinn. "It's obvious you two don't need to show up at Theon's since you're getting drunk at high noon no less," he puffed.

"Except for Catia," Quinn said into the cup.

"Can you guys not do this right now? We're almost to the palace." Rinn looked at them both, and they looked at Rinn but said nothing. "Okay, good. I'm glad you're both—"

"We never agreed to anything!" they said simultaneously.

"Shit," Rinn rolled his eyes and cracked the reigns, bringing the horses back to a trot. The trio made their way toward Theon's palace, and the golden fields slowly changed into green pastures with horses and cows grazing away. Rinn began to think to himself, *I have absolutely no idea what to tell Theon. It's my duty to keep Catia safe. Would I be going against my pledge to Theon if I keep my power and my identity a secret? It's not like I have much of a choice though.* He turned around and looked at Quinn. "Quinn, you said the empire is evil and that they came here from another realm, right?"

"That's correct. Good to know you can listen," Quinn replied sarcastically.

"So somewhere there is a way into their world. Wouldn't that be the case?" Rinn handed the reigns to Soko and turned around, then he pulled out a wooden bowl and poured it full of water. "Shouldn't we be able to go there too?" he queried as he sipped from the bowl.

"I've never thought about it like that. We were having enough trouble trying to push them back during the war. What do you think, Soko?" Quinn added.

"I'm sorry, I wasn't listening, but I know it's important," he said with his brows raised.

"Do you think we could go to the underworld?" Quinn said irritably.

"Why would we want to go where those hellish fuckers came from exactly?" he inquired in shock.

"Because we have the Satrium stone. Well, I mean we don't actually *have* it, but it's in our realm, so who's to say there isn't another stone of opposite power in theirs?" Rinn added while sipping from his bowl.

"And you continue to amaze me, Rinn! You're a genius!" Quinn grabbed Rinn's face and stretched it out. "You're definitely your father's son," Quinn added, still pulling on his face.

"Was he smart?" said Rinn through his stretched face.

"No, but your faces stretch the same." Quinn grinned and ruffled his hair. "But seriously, I see more and more of him in you each day, Rinn," Quinn added as he smiled and yanked Rinn's hair.

"Why do you do that shit for?" Rinn snapped.

"Just cause you're *so smart*," Quinn replied sarcastically.

"You two are an odd combo," Soko said into his cup, sipping mead.

"You have no idea how many times he's done this to me," retorted Rinn as he downed the rest of his water and put his bowl back in his bag. "It's practically normal at this point."

"I know the feeling there, I had to train the dipshit." Soko slurped out his last drink of mead and gulped it down.

"You trained Quinn?" Rinn asked in shock.

"Yup, since he was younger than you. Weren't you listening earlier?" Soko said casually.

"Since I was twelve," Quinn said, staring up at the sky.

"And he's *always* been a pain," Soko said, rolling his eyes.

"I thought you said we were close to the palace," Quinn whined.

"Yeah, we should be there by evening at the latest. Also give me time to sort it all out in my head, and I'll likely remember everything you told me," Rinn explained as he took off his cloak and tossed it in the back of the wagon. "But if we don't have any more stops, we should be there when the first sun touches the horizon." Rinn looked to the sky to judge how much they had left to travel and began thinking to himself, *I should be there in two hours at this pace. At least I'm not walking again, that would be dreadful.* As they ventured on, Rinn noticed something; all the animals had fallen silent. He looked over to Soko. "We need to stop for a moment."

"Why is there someone else?" asked Soko as he drew the horses to a stop.

"Do you hear anything at all?" Rinn looked at them both and waited for an answer.

"I don't even hear any birds," Quinn added in, looking around suspiciously.

"We shouldn't let our guard down. I get the feeling someone is following us again," Rinn scanned the area, looking for any signs as Soko cracked the reigns and brought the horses back to a gate.

"Do you think it's one of the exploding guys?" Quinn inquired as he scanned the area.

"No, I don't feel any kind of evil presence, just a really shitty smell," Rinn replied, flaring his nostrils. "Let's just keep moving. We'll find out who it is soon enough. There's a long bridge ahead." Rinn munched on a piece of beef jerky as they approached the bridge. It was long and narrow, so there was only just enough room for a single wagon to fit, but there were sections designed to spin for turning wagons around. The river was shallow all the way across, and the bridge wasn't very high off the river, but they still had to move slowly as the horses would likely give out otherwise. As they made their way across, Rinn looked into the clear water watching the fish swim by, following the river all the way to the horizon. The gentle sounds of the flowing river echoed in Rinn's ears. He smelled the refreshing river air and sighed.

"You must love life, boyo," Soko patted Rinn on the shoulder.

"I love this world and everything in it too," Rinn said as he watched birds play in flight. "I want to protect everyone and everything."

"There you go, sounding like your father again," said Quinn as he ruffled up Rinn's hair.

"Can't you do that *after* we get across this narrow ass bridge?" Soko snapped nervously.

"Why so nervous? Can't you swim?" Quinn said with a mischievous grin.

"I'm just not particularly fond of water, is all," Soko said tensely.

"*Raaargh!*" Quinn squalled as he threw Soko from the wagon into the river.

"*You feckin'dirty ngwad, I can't feckin' swim!*" Soko screamed in panic, flailing his arms and legs in a desperate attempt to get back to the bridge. Meanwhile, Rinn stepped into the river and grabbed Soko by the hand.

"Just stand up you, old dafty dingwad," he said laughing, which caused Quinn to cackle.

"Oh, go ahead and have a laugh at the expense of the elderly," Soko spat out. "I hope you both fall in a pile of cow shit," he said with a serious look.

"You're too old to be elderly. You're just ancient," Quinn added in a fit of laughter.

"I'm not that old. I'm still in me prime," Soko replied as he wrung out his clothes over Quinn's head, revealing he was quite fit despite his age.

"But you've had gray hair since we met," Quinn shook the water off his head, slinging it over both of his companions. "Besides, I think you should have a bath anyway, you smell like fish." Quinn chuckled.

"I didn't stink till you threw me in the water, and by the way, that isn't how you treat your master where I come from." Soko smacked Quinn with his hat, which was still thoroughly soaked.

"You stunk well before I gently tossed you into the stream. Now you're just a little moist," Quinn replied impishly.

"Shut yer trap before I stitch it up, ya feckin' assmonger." Soko's face turned crimson, and a vein started to pop out in his neck as he blew through his beard in frustration. "Yer both just the same with yer feckin' asinine shithead ways."

"You're cute when you're mad, Ko-Ko," said Quinn as he petted Soko's head.

"Just you wait, ya feckin shitheads," Soko mumbled under his breath.

"We're across Helmfast river, so I'll go on foot from here. Meet me where the road forks in about an hour's time." Rinn hopped off and started jogging into the trees.

"Does he ever use roads?" Soko turned to Quinn and gestured for him to move to the front.

"Nope. He says he doesn't see the point when straight lines are faster," Quinn said, stepping over into the seat.

"He said where the road forks in an hour, so should we get moving?" Soko poured another cup of mead and drank it straight down. "Ah, that's tasty stuff,"

"Let's go then." Quinn took the reins, and they were off. "I just hope he didn't forget about us being followed."

CHAPTER 3

A CROSSING OF FATES

Rinn kept running through the trees. *I'm almost there, just a bit farther,* he thought to himself. Suddenly, a young man covered in blood and dirt burst through the bushes and tackled Rinn to the ground "What's—?"

"Shhh, be quiet. Just trust me, stranger, or that thing will hear us," the man whispered.

"What thing?" whispered Rinn. The man pointed into the trees, in the same direction Rinn was running. Rinn's eyes widened in fear when he saw the giant monster the stranger spoke of. Its skin was the same green as the trees, and it was the size of three men or better. It seemed to walk at a snail's pace through the forest, but a dark power was emanating from its body. "What in the name of the gods is that foul giant?"

"That's a demon. I'm not sure what kind, but it's dangerous. He ate my men." The man's eyes grew hollow as he said this, which let Rinn know what happened. "He would've eaten you as well had I not stopped you in time."

Rinn sniffed the air. "Ugh, that thing smells like shit." He took a piece of his cloak and ripped it, then tied it around his face. "So how do we kill it? Do we cut off its head or cut out its heart?"

"It doesn't matter what you do if you don't have a sword made from Solinius steel. That's the only way to kill a demon," the man kept his eyes on the monster.

"Is this made from Solinius?" Rinn pulled out his sword slowly to avoid making any sounds and handed it to the man.

"This is beautiful," he replied as he held Rinn's sword and studied it closely. The curve of the blade was like looking at the crescent moon, and it had a pattern along the cutting edge that resembled a stormy sea. The edge disappeared entirely, and a ridge along the back of the blade showed its strength. "Have you ever put it in the light of the two suns?"

"Yes, why do you ask?" replied Rinn.

"What happens when you do?" he inquired.

"It turns blue," Rinn replied blatantly.

"Then we have a shot. We both have Solinius weapons. Do you know how to fight?" The man turned to look at Rinn, but he was already gone. *Where'd that guy run off to?* the man thought to himself. He looked at the demon and saw Rinn sprinting toward it at full speed.

"*Raaarghh!*" Rinn screamed as he slid between the demon's legs, causing it to swing with devastating speed. Rinn jumped and flipped out of the way. *It's so fast, but I can do this! I can't let it get any closer to Catia or Theon. It's already too close for comfort*" he thought to himself. The demon looked at Rinn and cracked a twisted smile.

"Another meal has come my way. I wonder if this one will scream as much as the last bunch," the demon snatched at Rinn, just missing his cloak.

"You can speak!" Rinn exclaimed as he jumped back, putting distance between them. "Do you have a name, demon? Or should I just call you demon?" Rinn took his stance and stared down his blade at the monster.

"A name? A name. It's been a while since my food ask me any questions. *Ahahaha!*" the demon's laugh was so loud it made Rinn's ears ring. "You can call me Roujin for all I care," he replied with a stomp, shaking the ground.

"Roujin, huh?" Rinn looked the demon in the eyes and smiled, which caused Roujin to frown. "I'm not your next meal. I'm here to slay you so those you killed can rest in peace, you filthy monster!"

"I'll show you who is in power here, boy!" Roujin's voice boomed with power as he raised his fist to crush Rinn. He charged with unthinkable speed for his size and smashed the ground where Rinn stood "Ha! Now let's see how you—"

"Ha-ya!" cried Rinn as he swooped down from above and beheaded the demon. He watched as his body went limp, and the light faded from his crimson eyes. Rinn looked down at the monster as the light left its eyes. He looked at his hand and made a fist. *I can use it now. When I think about the feeling I had when I killed that eagle, I can use the power.*

"What were you thinking, you fool?" the stranger scolded. "That thing had the strength of twenty men, and you just go in screaming? Are you an idiot or something?"

"Well, you said we had a shot, so I just went for it," Rinn stated blatantly.

"Are you fucking crazy?" the man said in shock.

"Well, one of us is. What's your name?" Rinn smiled. "Mine is Rinn."

"I'm Tusk. I slay demons like the one you just killed," he folded his arms and snorted.

"So you know about demons too, huh?" Rinn asked as he sheathed his sword.

"I wish I had never found out they existed, but I didn't have a say in the matter when they killed my family. It's my first memory." He looked down and sighed.

"I'm sorry. I never had a family." Rinn pulled his hood over his head. "I have to be going now." He started to head off but was stopped by his new acquaintance.

"Wait, do you think we could travel together for a while? That thing busted me up pretty bad." As soon as Tusk finished speaking, he coughed up blood and fainted.

Rinn rushed to catch him but was too late, and Tusk fell on his face. He picked him up and carried him on his shoulders as he sprinted through the trees. *You're not as heavy as the eagle friend, don't worry. Theon will help you.* Rinn ran as fast as he could until he busted out of the trees and into an open field of flowers on rolling hills. He looked to the top of the closest hill and spotted Theon's palace, a white beacon in the sunlight. Its white walls and pillars glistened like a lake in the suns' light. Rinn took off and sprinted up the hill. He ran until his lungs were burning and kept pushing until he made it to the gate.

"*Someone please help! It's Rinn! I've an injured man with me!*" As Rinn finished, the gate swung open, and Theon stepped out.

"What's wrong, my boy? Is he dying?" Theon helped get the man off Rinn's shoulders and helped them inside.

"I'm not sure, My Lord. There was a demon that killed and ate all his men and almost him. I had no idea he was injured when I killed it," Rinn replied.

"You slew the demon?" Theon asked in shock.

"Yes, My Lord. It was no trouble at all," Rinn said calmly.

"What made you help this man?" Theon handed the man over to his servants, and they took him away to look after his wounds.

"He saved me as I was coming to answer your summoning, My Lord." Rinn took a knee as he said this. "There's something I must tell you in private, Lord Theon."

"I see." Theon scratched his beard and ran his hands through his long, flowing blond hair. "Very well, let us go to my council room."

"Yes, My Lord." Rinn stood and followed Theon into the palace. The two of them ventured through the magnificent halls of stone and came to a small room with a circle of chairs but no table.

"What's on your mind, my boy? It must be serious for you to want to discuss it in private." Theon shed his robe and hung it on his chair before he sat down.

"You must answer me first, My Lord. I'm sorry," Rinn stared at the floor, and his hands began to tremble *I have to tell him what I am,* he thought to himself.

"What is it, son? You're worrying me." Theon placed his hand on Rinn's shoulder and looked at him with concern.

"What do you know of the great war that happened before I was born?" Rinn asked nervously.

"I know the wrong side won. I wouldn't call it a war though," Theon replied plainly.

"I-I'm a Drumaulian. I didn't know until yesterday." Rinn closed his eyes and waited for Theon to speak.

"Well, then I can assume you're more than capable of keeping my daughter safe. I already knew what you are because I knew your parents, Rinn. Gods, you can be dense." Theon shook his head and smiled. "You're definitely your father's son, my boy."

"Why am I the only one who didn't know I was something else?" Rinn clenched his fists and gritted his teeth in frustration. "I feel like my whole life has been one big lie." Theon wrapped his arms around him and embraced him.

"Because we had to protect our only hope." Theon squeezed him tightly. "Your father wanted it this way. But there isn't much I can say beyond that," he added with a smile as he stepped away.

"Thank you, My Lord. Did you know my father?" Rinn looked up to Theon.

"Not as well as I would've liked. I only knew him by reputation," Theon replied with a wave of his hand.

"I see," Rinn turned and bowed. "How may I serve you today, Lord Theon?"

"Catia will tell you she summoned you, not me. I've no idea what is in that girl's head. You'd be wise to tread lightly." Theon chuckled.

"And where can I find Lady Catia?" inquired Rinn.

"She's outside somewhere." Theon motioned for Rinn to go find her.

"I'll be on my way then." Rinn turned and headed back outside. *Theon knew. Catia probably doesn't know because she's a few years younger than me. I'll ask Quinn before I tell her just to be certain.* He headed through the courtyard and stopped by the fountain. It had a statue of Drumaul in the center wearing his armor, as decorative as it was protective. His sword looked a lot like Rinn's, but it was much longer. *I guess I should pay more attention to things,* he thought to himself as he turned and passed under an archway, then he spotted Catia smelling flowers. "My Lady Catia, how may I serve you?"

"You can start by explaining why you've been gone for three months! And what gave you all those scars?" To Rinn, Catia's voice was like listening to the voice of the goddess of love, whereas everyone else heard only harsh demands from an impatient, spoiled, hot-tempered little girl with fiery red hair and all the beauty in the land. She was about a head and a half shorter than Rinn, but she had a temper like Drumaul himself.

"I was hunting, my lady. I didn't mean to cause you any strife," he replied with a slight bow.

"And the scars?" she said with her arms folded.

"I ran into a pack of dire lykaons. I barely got away." He said, looking off to the sky.

"Well, no more hunting by yourself! How are you supposed to be my guard if you're dead!" Her voice was harsh, but Rinn knew she wouldn't be this way if she didn't care about him.

"With the way you're talking to him, I'm surprised he even comes back." Theon walked up and patted Rinn on the shoulder. "I told you to tread lightly, my boy."

"And what is *that* supposed to mean?" Catia's face started to turn red with rage, and she looked at Rinn for an answer.

"I don't know what I'm supposed to say," Rinn muttered nervously.

"Well, my boy, has she told you why you were summoned?" Theon chuckled.

"She hasn't told me yet, My Lord." Suddenly, Catia grabbed Rinn by the arm and dragged him away from Theon, then they started toward the outer gate "Catia, where are you—?"

"Shut it!" she snapped.

"Yes, my lady." Rinn never knew what was going through her mind, but he also knew just to go along with whatever she said, or he'd have to face her wrath. She pulled him by the arm until they were in the wheat fields outside the palace and stopped.

"Now are we all alone?" she asked, facing away from Rinn. He scanned the area with his eyes and ears then turned to her.

"I think so. I don't hear anyone else around. What's going on, Catia?" he queried, folding his arms.

"I overheard you talking with my father." She looked at him with eyes aglow and smiled. "Do you know what this means?"

"It means you're no longer safe with me. All I'll do is put you in more danger." Rinn looked at the ground and clenched his fists.

"No, you big dummy! We can get married!" She reached out for his hands, but Rinn stepped away.

"I'm not sure that's how it works, my lady," he replied, looking away from her.

"What do you mean? And why won't you look me in the eyes?" her voice trembled as she said this. "Don't you love me too?" she queried as tears started to roll down her cheeks.

"Of course I do. But I have my place and you have yours." He turned and wiped her tears away. "Don't cry just yet."

"But aren't you a Drumaulian?" She wrapped her arms around him and squeezed with all her strength. "Doesn't that make you eligible for us to be together?"

"I can't answer that." He ran his fingers through her hair. "I guess you heard I killed a demon then?"

"Yes, and I also heard it killed all that man's men." She looked up to him and smiled. "If you do anything that reckless again, I'll kill you," she added innocently.

"I understand, my lady. I'll do my best." Rinn patted her head and smiled.

"You damn well better." She buried her face into Rinn's chest. "You smell like blood. You always smell like blood."

"I'm sorry, I'll try to do something about it," he replied.

"Don't you two think you're a bit too close?" Theon inquired sternly with hollow eyes.

"My Lord Theon." Rinn pushed Catia off of him and took a knee "We were just—"

"I heard the whole conversation, Rinn," Theon said sternly. "Catia, are your feelings for him genuine?"

"Yes, Father," she replied, looking at the ground.

"And you feel the same about her, Rinn?" he barked.

"Yes, Lord Theon, sir, I—"

"*Enough!*" Theon boomed. "I guess I don't have a choice." Theon drew his sword and raised it above his head. "I, Theon, son of Leonon, Lord of Helmfast, hereby sentence you to death. Do you have any last words?"

"I'm sorry. May I serve you better in the next life." Rinn lowered his head and pulled his hood back.

"I see. Goodbye, Rinn, I'm sorry it had to end this way." Theon came down with his sword and stopped just before he touched Rinn then tapped both of his shoulders. "Hello, *Sir* Rinn, first knight of Helmfast."

"That wasn't funny at all!" Catia flew at her father in a fit of rage with tears streaming down her face, punching him in the chest all the while Theon was laughing. Meanwhile, Rinn was still on the ground, staring at the dirt, in shock.

"My Lord Theon, why have you given me this title?" Rinn queried in shock, staring at the dirt.

"I need to start building an army. Plus, I just can't stand to see her cry," Theon replied indifferently.

"An army? Why?" Rinn looked at him and tried to stand but collapsed.

"Rinn!" Catia kneeled and held his head in her lap. "What's wrong? Are you hurt?" She took off his shirt to check him for wounds and discovered a large bruise covering his chest, then Theon called for servants.

"I'm fine, really I am." He tried to raise himself but couldn't. "My ribs might not be though."

"Don't move, stupid!" Catia said with tears in her eyes. "Why don't you tell me when you're hurt?" She ran her hands over his chest and felt the broken bones. "By the gods, you're all busted up! How did this happen?"

"The force of the shockwave from Roujin's blows broke them, I guess. He managed to get one in on me after all." As he spoke, he coughed up blood and spat it out on the ground. "It's not that bad."

"The demon told you his name was Roujin?" Theon kneeled next to him and a servant helped him get Rinn to his feet. "To the infirmary with him, along with our strange guest."

"Yes, My Lord, why do you ask?" Rinn inquired.

"I've fought him once before is why. You were lucky to get away, let alone kill him. The gods must truly be watching over you, my boy," Theon patted him on the back, causing him to wince.

"I killed him not thirty paces into the trees just over there," Rinn strained out.

"I didn't think there would've been one so close. Especially *him*," Theon's eyes were full of terror, but he remained stoic.

"What happened between you and him?" Rinn winced in pain, and Catia put herself under his arm, sending the servant ahead.

"He killed my brother and almost got me while we were hunting when we were children." Theon's eyes grew hollow under his brow. "I'm glad it was you who faced him and not me, or I fear I would've fallen prey to him."

"I'm sorry to hear that, My Lord," he replied as he coughed up more blood then lost his footing, falling on the ground. "That felt wonderful."

"Rinn, stop being a baby and get up!" Quinn said, running up to the gate.

"All of his ribs are broken!" Catia snapped as she rushed over and slapped Quinn through the face, then she returned to Rinn. "Are you okay, my love?"

"I'm much better now that he got slapped." Rinn laughed and winced. "C'mon, Quinn, help me out here," he added, holding out his hand.

"Shit, you might actually be hurt. What happened to him, Theon?" Quinn picked him up and carried him into the courtyard.

"Remember that demon that ate my brother?" Theon asked.

"Roujin?" Quinn said in shock.

"He killed him, but he said nothing about getting hurt till he fell over coughing up blood," Theon added blatantly.

"How does everyone I know already know all these things?" Rinn said, trying to jerk free and causing Quinn to drop him.

"Oops," Quinn smiled and looked at Catia and back at Rinn. "So you're her love, eh?"

"Shut up for fuck's sake." Rinn picked himself up and walked into the infirmary. "I was just knighted by the way."

"Ha! That's a laugh!" Quinn smacked him on the back. "Soko is around here somewhere, so you'd best be watching out or he'll smack your ribs."

"Master Soko is here?" Theon started to look at the ceiling with a paranoid look on his face. "How long have you two been here anyway, Quinn?"

"About five minutes, and the fucker already disappeared," Quinn added.

"Why does everyone know each other?" Rinn laid himself down on a bed, and Catia kneeled next to him, then a servant gave him a small bottle of tonic.

"This will kill the pain," she said softly. "I'll be back with some bandages." She turned and walked by Quinn and grabbed him by the rear. "Good to see you, Quinny."

"Quinny? That's fantastic." Rinn smiled and drank the tonic down in one gulp and winced at the bottle. "That is the worst shit I've ever tasted."

"You buncha feckin' dandy dillies, where's yer feckin' cellar?" Soko's voice echoed across the courtyard, and Theon flinched then headed outside while Quinn followed suit.

"Now that we're alone for real." Catia kissed Rinn gently. Her lips were as soft as the finest silk. She held the kiss, and he placed a hand on her face. "I know we can get married now, *Sir* Rinn."

"Let's hold off for a little while longer, just until things settle down." He brushed her hair behind her ear and smiled. "I thought your father was gonna kill me." Suddenly, a curtain was pulled back, and a fair-faced man was laying on his side, facing the two of them.

"That's just precious, ain't it? Two lovebirds being two lovebirds." Tusk gave a playful snort and grinned.

"Good to see you're alive, Tusk. You look a lot younger when you aren't covered in blood." Rinn looked at him. "Have they treated your wounds?"

"Well, enough. Who's your lady friend, and what's your name again?"

"This is Lady Catia of Helmfast. And I'm Rinn," he replied politely.

"You're *Sir* Rinn evidently. I'm not sure what the whole sir thing means." He dug in his fingernails and scratched his face with his foot.

"Were you raised under a rock?" Catia looked at him with surprise.

"Pardon me, Lady Cat, but I wasn't raised by anyone. I grew up in the wild with the beasts," Tusk retorted.

"Just who do you think you are anyway?" Catia's face started to turn red, and she started to stand up, but Rinn held her hand.

"He saved me. Let him be," he said calmly.

"I don't like your new friend. He's rude, and he smells like a wild animal." Catia folded her arms and turned away from Tusk.

"I am right here, you know. You're not so friendly yourself, red," Tusk added.

"Tusk, tell us the story. I'd honestly like to know myself," Rinn said with his arm over his eyes.

"Hmph." He folded his arms and rolled over on his back. "I lost my family to a demon when I was a baby, so I don't remember much beyond it being horrible. A pack of dire lykaons raised me for about my first seven winters. When they took me on my first hunt, I killed a boar, and I made knives with the tusks. Then the pack leader brought me to a human village, and I've been a wanderer ever since." Tusk sighed.

"I'm sorry to hear that, honestly, but that's still no excuse not to bathe," Catia added as she covered her nose.

"She's so mean. How do you put up with her?" Tusk rolled over and looked at Rinn.

"She's not so bad." Rinn smiled at Catia, and she jabbed his ribs, causing him to grunt in pain.

"Not so bad! I'm the best thing that could've happened to you, idiot!" She bent over and put her breasts in his face. "Don't you agree, my love?"

"Yes, dear." Rinn stared at her breasts in awe as the servant came back with the bandages. Catia helped him sit up while the servant wrapped the bandages around him. "Did Quinny give you any trouble?"

"Something like that," the servant girl replied with a wink.

"Don't be gross, Millie," Catia said into her hands.

"Yes, Lady Catia. The same goes for you two." Millie walked back outside, and Rinn stood up and started to follow suit.

"Just where exactly do you think you're going?" Catia grabbed his arm and scowled at him.

"Well, I was going outside, if that's okay," he replied blatantly. "Do you want to come with me? I was going to ask Theon if we could be together." Rinn forced a smile through the pain.

"I think that's why he knighted you. Besides, you have broken ribs! You shouldn't even be standing right now." She held on to his arm in an attempt to keep Rinn still. Instead, he held Catia up off the ground, and he started walking around the courtyard.

"I still want to go talk to him. I don't feel right not doing it. Plus, it's really not that bad, I can hardly feel any pain." He walked through the flower garden when Rinn noticed how light Catia felt hanging on his arm. Then he felt how soft her hands were against his callused hands, and Rinn started to think, *I thought I was on death's door, but Theon knighted me instead. Was it to keep Catia safe, or was it because of something else? I guess it's a bit of both."*

"What're you thinking about?" Catia tiptoed over and kissed him on the neck. The softness of her lips sent chills down his arm. "Is it so important that you can't stop to look at me?"

"I was thinking about how I almost died five times today…also, how Lord Theon could have been my end." He looked down to her and smiled. "Your hair is so beautiful, Catia."

"Hush, it's awful. It's always like this, and it's so thick I can't even get a brush through it." She hid her face in Rinn's chest and held his locket in her hands. "You still have the charm I gave you?"

"I've never taken it off." He kissed her forehead gently. "It reminds me I've always got somewhere I belong." He patted her on the head and popped the locket open, revealing a large green stone radiating its own light as if it were a small flame. "I'm starting to think this charm is the only reason I'm alive."

"You're so sweet to me, but everyone else says you're coldhearted. Why do they say that?" she asked, looking up to him.

"I'm not sure I've ever killed a person, just beasts. I guess it's because I never speak to the people in town." Rinn shrugged and winced in pain.

"Well, I think you're the kindest man I've ever met. Not to mention that you're good to look at and not some troll." She stopped Rinn and pulled him off into the hedges.

"What are you dragging me off to do now?" Rinn chuckled, then Catia turned her back to him and wrapped his arms around her.

"Ah, this is why I summoned you here. I missed feeling your arms holding me. Do you remember the first time you held me?" She looked up to him with eyes of emerald lit aglow with love.

"You were drunk in Greyman's, and your father nearly had my head. You were trying to fight one of his barmen because he wouldn't serve you anymore drinks," Rinn replied blankly.

"I don't remember *that* part about it. But I do remember having a terrible pain in my head the next morning." She pouted as she turned her head away.

"Which is why your father explicitly says for you to not drink." Rinn smelled her hair as they watched the second sun set over the horizon and the first moon rose in its place. "My lady Catia?"

"Yes, Rinn?" She looked up to him with a smile that would melt the heart of anyone in the land.

"I love you," he said as he closed his eyes and looked down. Catia stepped away from him and turned around with tears of joy in her eyes.

"That's the first time you've actually said it since we met. Why did you have to wait so damn long?" She hung herself around his shoulders and kissed him deeply. Rinn gave a winced smile as she kissed him while he held her gently.

"I couldn't say it. Not until I knew we could be together." He kissed her gently then started to walk toward the palace.

"Where are you going?" She beckoned him to come back, and he looked at her with a smile.

"*We* have to go and talk to them. There's more news I have for your father." Rinn's eyes narrowed, and the two of them started walking.

"Okay, but I don't know why it can't wait until morning." She pouted and held onto his arm as the two of them walked through the door and into the dining hall where they found Theon staring at the ceiling with a dumbstruck look on his face. Rinn looked up to find Soko hanging from the rafters by his legs, doing his best to down a jar of wine.

"Come down from there master and give me back my wine! That's the most expensive one I can get!" Theon threw his arms up in the air in protest and looked at Rinn then pointed a finger at Soko. "He's fucking hopeless."

"If this wine is expensive, it's a feckin' rip-off. It tastes like the backside of a horse's balls." Soko threw the jar at Theon, and it busted on the floor. Then Soko was suddenly on the floor, standing in front of Rinn and Catia. "So you killed Roujin?"

"Yes. I can only guess you're the reason why Theon escaped," Rinn replied. "How's your nose?" he queried impishly.

"A lot better than your ribs!" Soko flicked his bandages, and Rinn grunted in pain. "Maybe you're not as dense as I first thought you were, boyo."

"Yes, he's the one who saved me," Theon added as he swept up the broken jar and smiled. "I see you two are still committed to being together."

"I want to marry him, Father," Catia stood her ground and looked at him with conviction.

"Aren't you a bit young for marriage? I don't mind you two being together, but the thought of my girl getting married just doesn't sit right with me." Theon swept the broken jar into a hatch in the floor that was filled with other broken items. "Waste of good wine."

"You wouldn't know a good wine if it jumped down your throat," Soko snapped.

"You mean we can be together?" Catia squeezed Rinn's arm in anticipation.

"Did I not just say that?" Theon sat down at the table and poured out a glass of wine. "Catia, would you excuse us? There's important matters to attend to."

"Yes, Father," Catia replied giddily as she curtsied and headed back outside while Rinn sat with Theon.

"Master Soko, please go and fetch Quinn and our guest." At these words, Soko vanished in what seemed like ash. "That never gets any less weird."

"Everything is weird to me." Rinn poured himself a glass and gulped it down. "That tonic made me thirsty," he poured a second glass and took another drink.

"I suppose you do deserve to know what's been going on." Theon poured more wine into Rinn's glass. "Mostly this was your father's idea, from my understanding. Like I said, I didn't know him as well as I would've liked to." Theon filled his own glass and set the bottle on the table.

"I see, I guess fate intervened with his plans for me." Rinn gulped down the second glass and noticed his hands were shaking. "I guess I'm still a little bit shocked from today."

"I can't say that I blame you. Meeting Roujin would affect anyone," Theon added as he looked down at his glass. "What's our guest's name?"

"His name is Tusk," Rinn replied as he took another sip of wine.

"Odd name but okay." Suddenly, Soko rematerialized in front of them, holding Quinn by the ear and gripping Tusk by the arm. The both of them were doing their best to get out of his grip.

"Who or what are you, and why did you drag me out of bed?" Tusk strained out.

"Because *he* said for me to fetch you two," Soko retorted as he plopped the two of them into a chair.

"Well, you didn't have to drag me away from my dear sweet Millie," Quinn said with his arms folded.

"And which one is she? You're fifth or tenth sweetheart you've been courtin' just today?" Soko snapped.

"I'm just having trouble deciding on one," Quinn replied innocently.

"What do *I* have to do with anything you fuckers are involved in? And why are you friends with this demon anyway?" Tusk inquired with disgust.

"I'm not a demon, ya feckin' halfwit!" Soko snapped, slapping him in the back of the head. "Now, my young students, I believe there's something to talk about." He placed his hands on both Quinn and Tusk's heads, making them sit still.

"Yes, there is. I believe the gods or fate itself has decided that we all come together on this day," Theon added as he stood and walked to the head of the table. "We must take action against Satrisia. Their heinous rule over our lands must end as soon as possible. Day after day, the innocent are being subjugated to torture just for the entertainment of the twisted people of the capitol. We must act before this evil spreads to our home." Theon took his seat and looked at his companions.

"You give a mighty good speech, but Rinn ain't nearly wise or strong enough to even think about starting a rebellion," Soko vanished and reappeared with a barrel of mead.

"How do you do that?" Rinn asked as he banged his head on the table. "I don't understand anything you guys do. Gods help me," he added as Tusk patted his head.

"You're not alone in that. This is way too much thinking for me," Tusk added, attempting to comfort Rinn.

"I told you that you weren't the only one with a few tricks, ya daft bull." Soko filled everyone's glasses with the mead, dashing any wine he found in them on the floor. "Nasty stuff, that is," he added as he spat on the wine he'd dashed out.

"You're wasting alcohol," Theon mumbled as he sipped the mead, then his eyes grew wide with delight. "That is the most flavorful drink I've ever had—and it's strong too!" He gulped the rest of it down and held his chest. "Oh my, that burns as it goes down." He sighed.

"You mean you've never had any of Greyman's mead, Lord Theon?" Rinn inquired as he downed his glass.

"I'll have to pay the old sot a visit." Theon poured another and swirled it in his glass. "What say you all to my request? Will you do whatever it takes to fight?"

"Of course, but we need more numbers, and we need to be able to trust everyone in command." Soko looked around the table and smiled. "It looks like we have our commanders already though," he added, looking at Quinn and Tusk.

"Commanders for what?" snapped Tusk. "I just slay demons. I'm not interested in fighting in some war." He started to stand, but Rinn grabbed his arm.

"Just hear them out. You can kill all the demons you want in this war," Rinn's icy eyes stared deep into Tusk's soul, and he took his seat. Then Tusk snatched his glass off the table and sniffed it.

"Why does this water smell funny?" Tusk continued to study the mead.

"Just drink it, it'll make you feel good," Soko said as he grabbed Tusk by the nose and poured it down his throat, causing Tusk to cough and gag.

"That's definitely not water!" Tusk said, holding his throat.

"You mean to tell me you've never had alcohol before?" Soko said in shock.

"What's *alhocal?*" Tusk said in confusion.

"Al-co-hol. The gods' gift to the world? Mead, brandy, porter?" Soko poured him another glass. "Wash it down with this." He put the cup in Tusk's hand.

"The commanders," Theon added sternly, "are for the army we will raise together to defeat the Shoindal. They are all of you. I don't trust anyone else enough to even consider them."

"Okay, so basically we're supposed to raise an army from farmers and blacksmiths?" Quinn asked.

"If that's what we have to work with, then yes." Theon's voice showed conviction, letting everyone know he wouldn't take no for an answer. Rinn looked around the table and noticed how everyone's faces had grown somber at the thoughts of war.

"I say we get started first thing tomorrow on recruiting every able-bodied man from all the surrounding villages!" Rinn exclaimed enthusiastically.

"Unfortunately, the situation is not that easy. See, there's a many number of things that have to be put in order before we can start recruiting people," Theon stated as he poured his third glass of mead.

"Oh. Well, what do we need to do first?" Rinn looked at Theon and sipped from his glass.

"We have to get enough weapons and armor to supply our troops, and we have to be sure all of it is made from Solinius or there won't be a point in fighting them." Theon looked around the table and smiled. "You wouldn't happen to know a master smith around these parts would you?" Everyone but Rinn looked down and shook their heads.

"I know a pretty good blacksmith. I know he can forge Solinius because he made my sword. The only problem is he's a few towns over." Rinn scratched his face and looked around to see that everyone was staring at him. "What? Is there something on my face?"

"I guess you'll have to go get him and convince him to come forge the weapons and armor." Theon looked over to Rinn with a smirk "That's an order, Sir Knight."

"Well, *he* isn't going anywhere without me," Catia barked as she swung the door open. "I think it'll be a nice change of pace," she added as she put her hands on her hips.

"Catia dear, don't you think it's a bit dangerous?" Theon pleaded, attempting to sway his daughter.

"I'll be fine. Rinn is going to be there too. I know he'll keep me safe," Catia wrapped her arms around Rinn. "Isn't that right, darling?"

"I'll do my best, if it's okay with your father," Rinn replied.

"Master Soko, would you accompany Rinn and my daughter to give me peace of mind?" Theon asked with concern.

"Of course, young blood. I'll go to the ends of time and beyond for every one of my students," Soko replied as he downed his glass and smiled.

"Thank you, Quinn. I need you to stay here with me so we can come up with a plan," Theon added. "And Tusk?"

"Hmmm?" Tusk looked over with his eyes.

"What will you do?" Theon inquired.

"Is it up to me?" he queried as he turned his head toward Theon.

"You can decide on what you do," Theon replied plainly.

"I believe I'll go with Rinn and see if this is gonna be worth all the trouble I'll be getting into," he added as he downed his glass.

"Your help is appreciated," Rinn patted Tusk on the shoulder. "Lord Theon, when will supper be ready?"

"It shouldn't be too much longer. Go ahead and rest up until then. I'll have Millie or one of the others come find you." Theon stood and headed through the door and down the hall with Quinn in tow.

"Rinn, who is that man over there?" Catia whispered into his ear.

"That is Soko the Soulless," Rinn said with a smile.

"But how come Father calls him master?" At these words, Soko was an inch away from her, looking down with his eyes of coal, causing Catia to step behind Rinn.

"What's the matter? Are you afraid of a poor old man like myself?" Soko inquired as he leaned over the two of them.

"Soko, that's enough," Rinn said sternly.

"Don't worry, young Catia dear, I won't let anything happen to my goddaughter." Soko patted her head and vanished.

"I'm starting to feel like his eyes weren't even poisoned." Rinn turned and started heading outside with Catia clinging to him. "And I'm starting to feel like this is gonna be a *long* trip."

"What's that supposed to mean?" Catia snapped, scowling up at Rinn.

"Nothing at all, dear," Rinn said, smiling while patting her on the head.

"Okay!" She kissed Rinn on the cheek. "Let's say we go to the fields! I've got a present for you." She tugged on his hand and smiled.

"I wonder what I'm in for this time." Rinn rolled his eyes as Catia pulled him toward the gate, and she brought him to the spot where they were before. Catia gave a long whistle, and something started rustling through the grass toward the two of them.

"By the gods, it's something *alive*!" Rinn took a step back as it approached.

"Calm down, it's little." Catia crouched down with her arms held out. "Come here, boy!" Suddenly, a small, fluffy silver ball with legs jumped out of the wheat and into Catia's arms, then she stood up and reached it out to him. "See? It's an itty-bitty!"

"That's a dire lycaon pup, Catia," Rinn said blankly. "Where'd you even find it?"

"In a cave gnawing on some bones," she replied blankly, still holding it in his face. "Go on, take it, he's all yours. Just like you're *all mine*," she added suggestively. Rinn took the puppy in his hands and studied it by holding it by its neck and checking all its teeth and feet.

"You just haphazardly walked into a dire lycaon den, grabbed a puppy, and left?" Rinn scowled at Catia while he held the puppy like a baby. "And what, pray tell, made you think that was a good idea?"

"Well, it was all alone in there, and it looked so helpless, so I thought you'd want to keep it." She looked down and twiddled her thumbs. "You look adorable right now."

"Wha—?" Rinn's face turned red in embarrassment. "Now my face matches your hair."

"Hey, that isn't funny! My hair isn't that red." She pushed him playfully, and the pup growled.

"You're right, it's way redder." Rinn turned and started back toward the palace. "C'mon, I bet this thing is hungry."

"Okay, but don't I get anything as payment?" Catia looked at him, still twiddling her thumbs.

"Hmmm. Is this what you mean?" He leaned in and kissed her deeply, causing the pup to growl again. Then the two of them laughed as they headed back to the palace. "At least it has blue eyes. The yellow eyes freak me out."

"Just like you," Catia held his arm, and they ventured back through the courtyard.

"Miss Catia! Rinn! Supper is on the table!" Millie's sweet voice rang from the window.

"C'mon, let's go eat. I've not had a hot meal in months." Rinn looked at her, and she nodded. Then the two of them headed back inside through the main hall. They ventured through the bloodwood arches and stone walls, then the smell of food hit Rinn's nose. *Oh, it smells so good! I wonder what they made this time,* he thought to himself. Finally, the two of them came into the dining hall where Tusk was already stuffing his face with a banquet of food laid before him. There were roasted chickens, quail, and half a bull with potatoes laid in the ribs with fresh salads laid out around the meats. "A true feast, thank you for the food!" Rinn exclaimed as he took his seat.

"Millie and the girls *always* cook more when you're here," Theon added as he approached them from behind.

"Lord Theon, look!" Rinn held the pup by its neck, and it started wagging its tail at Theon. "It's a dire lycaon."

"The goddess Fitra has blessed you with a hunter." Theon scratched its chin, and they all took their seats at the table.

"I see you started without us, Tusk," Rinn said, smiling as he made his plate.

"I've not had any food in two weeks," Tusk replied with his mouth full.

"How do you manage to survive like that for two weeks?" Quinn inquired as he took his seat.

"That does seem mighty odd indeed," Soko added as he appeared behind Tusk.

"Would you please stop doing that?" Tusk snapped. "Haven't you ever heard of using a damn door?" Tusk glared at him and growled.

"That's not as much fun now, is it?" Soko retorted as he took his seat and started piling up his plate. "Is someone under the table?" Soko peeked under to find the pup chowing down on a rack of cow ribs. He rose up and saw Rinn tossing it his scraps as he finished his food. "Is that your tiny death bringer under there?"

"Yeah. Catia gave it to me," Rinn replied as he started to dish up a second plate. "Have the servants ate yet?"

"We've already eaten, Rinn," Millie responded as she lured Quinn away with his plate. "You're gonna come with me," she said flirtatiously.

"I suppose everything is to your liking?" Theon said, pointing a bone at Rinn.

"Father, don't point with your food," Catia scolded. She was the only well-mannered one at the table, eating with utmost care and sophistication.

"Leave me be," Theon said with a mouthful.

"So damn good!" Tusk added as he ripped a leg off one of the chickens.

"It's quite delicious indeed," Soko added.

"Yes, it's truly marvelous," Rinn replied. As they all ate together, Rinn felt at ease for the first time since he started his journey. *Today has been one of the most fucked-up days I've ever had. I'm exhausted. Everyone else doesn't seem bothered by all of this,* he thought to himself as he looked around the table and noticed nobody was smiling but Catia. *She must not know Theon intends to start another war.*

"Please excuse me," Rinn said as he finished his second plate. He stood and headed through the main hall and down a flight of stairs into the cellar with his pup in tow.

"Rinn! Wait for me!" Catia called out. "Is there something wrong?"

"It's nothing, I just needed to walk off my food before bed." He turned and watched her walk down the stairs. *I feel like I'm dreaming,* he thought to himself. "Catia, will you slap me please?"

"Why? Did you do something mean?" She put her hands on her hips and raised a brow.

"I just feel like none of this should be happening." He leaned on the wall and sank to the floor, putting his head between his knees. "Just yesterday I thought your father would kill me for *thinking* of you in a romantic way. Now it's like he couldn't care any less. In fact, it's almost as if he's happy about it," he added, scratching his head in frustration.

"That's because he *is* happy about it," Catia sat on her knees in front of him and put her arms around him, burying his head into her breasts. "You're thinking too much again, my love. Just try to relax." She held him there for a moment, stroking his hair. Rinn could hear her heart beating, and he placed his hand on her face. She nuzzled into his hand and smiled. "Your hands have always been so rough, but I've never felt anything so gentle."

"You're amazing, Catia." Rinn sighed in relief. "I wonder what sort of strange thing will happen next," he added, rubbing his eyes.

"Only the gods know." She pulled herself closer to him. "I could stay here like this forever," she added as she kissed his head.

"Here in the cold, damp cellar?" Rinn started to stand and felt a pain shoot through his chest. "Well, I think they're definitely broken. Could you show me to a room please? I'd like to lay down on something soft."

"I know just the place." She led him back up the stairs and through the palace. The two of them made their way to a spiral staircase, and she led him up to the second floor. "Right here." She flung open the first door and stepped into the room. Rinn stepped in and realized she'd led him into her room, and a feeling of terror came over him.

"I can't sleep here! Theon will cut my throat!" He held his neck and backed out of the room. Suddenly, Catia was right in front of him, looking up with big green eyes that could melt the heart of any beast or man in the whole world.

"You mean you won't share a bed with me?" She pressed her breasts against his chest and put her hands in his.

"That's *exactly* what I'm saying. Even though it makes me cringe." Rinn stared straight up at the ceiling.

"Well, well, well, what do we have here?" A child's voice rang from down the hall. "Is this something I should tell Father about?"

"Father already knows about us, Bjorn. You're missing out on supper by the way." Catia rolled her eyes and looked down at her little brother. He was the spitting image of his father with golden hair and big golden eyes filled with wonder.

"So you're courting a commoner with Father's permission? Like *that* would ever happen." Bjorn looked up at the two of them and smiled mischievously.

"Actually, your dear old dad just made me a knight, little warrior, so I'm not a commoner anymore," Rinn said as he ruffled Bjorn's hair. Rinn had always thought of Bjorn as a little brother, and Bjorn thought the same of him.

"I see. All is well then. I'm gonna go and eat. Ooh, a puppy!" Bjorn picked up the pup and let it lick his face all over. "Haha! You're a fun one. Is he mine?"

"No, I got him for Rinn because you keep turning your pets loose." Catia snatched the pup and Bjorn scowled.

"Fine then." He scurried down the stairs, leaving the two of them alone.

"Can you please let me use the usual room?" Rinn added as he stared at her breasts.

"Hmph. Fine, c'mon then." She led him to the end of the hall and into the guest room, which was still finely decorated with a large bed. "But I'm staying in here with you to be sure your wounds don't bother you so much," she added as she walked to the far side of the bed.

"Theon is gonna kill me for real this time," Rinn laid down slowly to avoid causing himself any pain.

"No, he won't. It's not like I'm letting you have me or anything." Catia crawled into the bed and laid down next to him, placing a hand on his chest. Then the pup started trying to jump on the bed but fell short, so it started to whine and pull on the sheets. "Aw, come here." She reached down and scooped it up, then it stumbled across the bed and flopped over at their feet.

"I wonder what I should name it." He rubbed his face in deep thought. "I know he's gonna be bigger than me someday, so he should have a fitting name."

"How's Cadius?" Catia said with her eyes closed.

"Let's see. Cadius." The pup remained still. "Guess it'll have to wait till he wakes up. I'm exhausted." He yawned, and Catia followed suit.

"I'm sleepy." She snuggled up to him and sighed. Rinn could feel her warmth rushing over him like water. *No matter what happens, I'll protect your life with my own. I pray to all the gods that I can keep this promise to my dying breath.* With this thought, Rinn fell into a deep sleep.

CHAPTER 4

THE FIRST STEP

Rinn woke to the sounds of birds singing and the first sun shining into his window. The crisp smell of dew wafted into the room. He looked around and saw that Catia had been by his side all night. She was sprawled out on the bed still in her dress with her hair covering her face. He took a deep breath and winced in pain.

"Catia, wake up, it's morning." He shook her, causing Cadius to wake up, and he jumped on Rinn's chest, which shot an intense pain through Rinn's body. "Gah!" Rinn coughed and blood spurted out, then he fell out of the bed with a thud.

"What's going on?" Catia rose up out of her slumber, hair like a blazing fire. "Rinn? Where are you? He better not have—"

"I'm down here," Rinn said into the floor. She rolled across the bed and poked her head over the edge, and her eyes lit up with delight.

"Good morning, love." She crawled out of bed and helped him to his feet. "Are you hurting?" She looked at him with concern.

"All thanks to Cadius." Rinn scooped up the pup, and they headed for the door. "Is there any more of that tonic Millie gave me? It was rancid, but it definitely let me breathe a lot better," he said as he felt up and down his chest, feeling his broken ribs.

"We'll just have to go ask her. I wonder what's for breakfast," Catia sniffed the air and bounced her way down the hall with Rinn.

"I'm more worried about my lungs at this point. I coughed up blood again." Rinn walked down the stairs with her, and they headed back outside. "Millie! I could use some help please!" Millie's head popped around the corner, and she rushed over to him with her long, flowing brown hair almost dragging the ground.

"What's the matter?" She looked the two of them over suspiciously. "There's been some mighty sneaky business happen between you two. Spill it!" she demanded as she put her hands on her hips, tapping her foot.

"We just slept in the same bed, nothing happened," Catia replied as she blew her hair out of her eyes. "He needs some tonic," she added, frowning at her hair. The three of them headed to the infirmary, and Millie shuffled through all the tiny bottles and snatched one filled with a black, ink-like liquid.

"Drink this, and you won't be needing anymore tonics." She plugged Rinn's nose and poured it into his mouth. It flowed slowly like tar, and his face cringed at the flavor as he gulped it down with a gag.

"I thought the tonic was rancid! That's the worst thing I've ever tasted! What was that stuff?" Rinn asked, holding his throat.

"Healing potion I got from some caravan. It'll fix those broken ribs." She turned and headed back outside in a rush.

"Well, that's just grand now, isn't it?" Soko added as he appeared in the doorway. "You two make quite the pair." He folded his arms and raised his brows. "When will we be off? Tusk has been waiting for you two to wake up," he added, glancing over at Tusk who was hanging upside down off the back of the wagon, staring at the three of them intensely.

"We can leave when Theon's had the opportunity to see us off. Where is he?" Rinn started taking off his bandages and saw the bruises were growing smaller and smaller by the second. "At least it wasn't poison."

"I don't see how those potions of hers work." Catia watched in amazement as his wounds were healed almost instantly.

"Well, whatever the case, we've got to get a move on to the smithy so he can forge all the weapons we need." Soko turned and headed toward the gate.

"Right. Let's go find Theon." Rinn tossed his bandages into the fire pit, grabbed his shirt off the cot, and the two of them followed Soko to the gate.

"Rinn, is there something going on? Why do you need weapons?" Catia pulled on his shirt and looked up to him with concern.

"I'll let your father answer that question. I don't feel like it's my place." He turned and saw Soko had already prepared the wagon for their trip. A tarp was draped over the back in case of rain, and he had it all loaded up. Tusk was rummaging around in the back, muttering under his breath and tossing things out of his way.

"Where's my fucking axes, you crazy old coot?" Tusk snapped.

"They're up front where they can't hurt the mead," Soko retorted.

"This is gonna be just *wonderful.*" Rinn rolled his eyes and picked up his sword from the wagon then put it on his belt. "Catia, are you sure you wanna—?"

"Don't even *try* to talk me out of it now. I've already made my mind up." She crawled into the back of the wagon and sat down on the sleeping bags that had been laid out to make extra seats in the wagon.

"She's right," Theon concurred as he walked into the gate from outside. "She's as stubborn as her mother was." Catia looked down and turned away at this remark.

"We'll return in a month's time at the most. I'll make sure we have a safe journey, you have my word." Rinn patted Theon on the shoulder and smiled. Theon nodded and walked around to the front of the wagon while Rinn climbed in the back with Catia.

"Master, please be careful and stay close to the roads when you make camp." Theon held Soko's wrist and looked at him with golden eyes. "I couldn't forgive myself for letting her go if something was to happen."

"Naturally, my boy. I promise you she's in fine hands with Rinn alone. Though I'm not so certain about this halfwit." He looked over at Tusk who was sniffing some jerky like it was something he'd never seen. "He's such an odd young man," he added, shaking his head.

"Well, I'll let you be on your way then. Catia, my lovely daughter, I'll be here when you return! I love you!" Theon turned away and headed back to the palace as the reins cracked, and they started moving.

"I love you too, Father!" she called back.

"This is just too weird," said Rinn. "Having you with me on the road, that is," he added as he turned to her.

"It does feel strange. I've never been no farther than the town of Helmfast, but you said the blacksmith was three towns over and that it'll be a month before we get back. Where's Cadius?" She looked around the back of the wagon for the pup and found him chewing away on a piece of jerky.

"He's gonna be a handful, I just know it." Rinn picked him up and held him up to his face. "Your name is Cadius, little one." The pup cocked its head to the side and wagged its tail.

"He's so cute!" Catia said as she scooted across the wagon. "I just can't get over it," she added as she started playing with Cadius.

"He's gonna be taller than me. You do realize a dire lycaon grows to be the size of a horse, right?" Rinn sat him down and Catia sat in his lap and pressed herself against him. "Oh gods…"

"What's wrong, love?" Catia queried, having no idea what she was doing to him, and she looked up with innocent eyes.

"Every time I turn around, you two are pawing at each other." Tusk puffed as he opened the tarp to the front. "You're like watching two crimlochs during spring." Catia's face turned red with embarrassment, and Rinn followed suit.

"What does he mean, Rinn?" Catia inquired innocently.

"It's nothing, don't worry about it." Rinn shifted and held her in his arms. "Quinn is probably gonna get Millie pregnant while we're gone," he added jokingly.

"*Ha!*" Soko cackled and turned around. "I bet you're right!" He cracked the reigns and brought the horses to a trot, and the party made their way back to the crossroads by the river. "Which way?" he called out.

"Go right here, and we'll come up on the first town by night-fall," Rinn answered. Soko nodded, and then they made their way down the road. He looked out of the back of the wagon, and Catia crawled over to the back of the wagon and watched as her home grew smaller and smaller in the distance. She smiled as it disappeared and sighed.

"I can't believe I'm actually here with you." She looked down and started to cry.

"Catia, what's wrong?" Rinn placed a hand on her shoulder, caressing it gently.

"I-it's just that Mother would've never let me go anywhere. But I'm so happy I can see the world. She was always so strict with me, telling me how a lady should act and all that." She wiped the tears away and smiled. "She'd be furious if she knew what I was doing now. I miss her so much." She broke down, and tears started streaming down her face. Rinn wiped the tears away, and she threw herself onto him, burying her face into his chest.

"I've never seen you cry before now." He held her tightly and stroked her hair. "I never even thought it was possible." He sat and let her cry until she stopped and fell asleep. "Okay, I'll let you sleep for a little while." He hopped out of the wagon and trotted up to the front. "Hey! Make some room!" He hopped up and sat in the front next to Tusk.

"So wagons are alive, right?" inquired Tusk.

"How long have you been living in the wild?" Rinn asked.

"Since I could walk. I don't even know how old I am or what day I was born. I can remember nineteen winters," Tusk replied as he picked at his toes.

"That's gross," Soko barked as he smacked Tusk on the back. "And no wagons are not alive for the tenth time," he added irritably.

"It moves and makes sounds! It has to be a tick, I mean it's got these horses in its mouth," he argued, sniffing the wagon. The three of them sat in silence, and Rinn reached in the back and poured them all a cup of mead, and they drank together without a word. As the second sun rose over the northern horizon, Tusk sniffed the air and gripped his axes.

"What is it?" Soko pulled his hat over his eyes. "Is someone coming?"

"I smell a crimloch, it's close," Tusk replied as he jumped off the wagon and sprinted down the road then dove into the river.

"What the fuck is this halfwit doing?" Soko looked at Rinn for an answer, but he shrugged and the two of them watched as Tusk climbed back out of the river holding a half-grown crimloch in his arms.

"It's nearly drowned!" He put it down and pressed on its chest and water spewed out of its mouth, and it jerked back to life, pouncing on him. Its fangs were already the size of daggers and protruded from either side of its mouth. It roared in his face, and he screamed back at it, causing it to take a step back—then it sat. Soko pulled the wagon to a stop and started to hop down, but Tusk halted him. "I saved you, now you owe me." He looked it in its ruby-red eyes, and it purred at him, flicking its tail.

"Does that thing *understand* you?" Rinn asked in shock. Catia popped her head out of the back and rubbed her head.

"What are you going on about anyways?" She rubbed her eyes, and Rinn pointed at Tusk who was already petting on the crimloch. "Is that…?"

"Yeah, he just pulled it out of the river, and I'm pretty sure it understands him," Rinn said as he hopped off the wagon and started toward them with Cadius in tow. The crimloch turned and flopped over while Tusk scratched its belly. "Well, it has a black mane that's starting to grow."

"They all have black manes…well, most of the time," Tusk replied as he grabbed the crimloch by the face. "I'm gonna call you Fang," the crimloch moaned and raised up.

"A fitting name with those big teeth of his. So can you talk to animals, or are you just a little crazy?" Rinn asked in disbelief.

"I can talk to them, but I don't understand anything they say back." Tusk walked to the back of the wagon. "In you go!" At these words, it trotted over and hopped into the wagon to everyone's astonishment.

"Well, I'm honestly done being surprised by things," Rinn said, throwing his arms in the air. He climbed up in the front, and Catia stepped over the seat and sat between Soko and Rinn.

"I'm not sitting with *that* thing." She pouted spitefully.

"I understand. Tusk, you're in the back. Keep your pet out of the meat or we'll starve." Rinn picked up Cadius then set him in the wagon, and he curled up in Catia's lap. Soko cracked the reigns, and they started moving again. *Things just keep getting weirder around here,* Rinn thought to himself. "Soko, how old are you?" Rinn queried suddenly.

"Why are you asking?" Soko replied, peeking out from under his hat.

"Because Quinn said you were old when you two met. I just remembered that," he added.

"I'm about four hundred years old now," he replied.

"What? Are you?" Catia asked in shock.

"I'm not a human like you, but I am mortal. I'm an Aesiri," Soko replied as he stared ahead.

"You're a servant to Aesirith? The goddess of death?" Catia asked as Tusk started to poke Soko in the back with the handle of his ax.

"So you're…"—Rinn guided Tusk's ax handle away and looked at Soko—"you're an agent of death?"

"Somewhat aye, I suppose I am." Soko's eyes grew hollow, and he looked down at the ground. "I understand if you feel differently about me."

"Nonsense, this is probably the coolest thing ever!" Catia blurted out. "You're a living relic, just like my Rinn." She gawked at him a little and smiled. "Sorry, I'm just trying to make you feel better."

"So he's yours then, eh?" Soko said with an impish grin, causing Rinn to blush.

"T-that's just not right," Rinn stuttered.

"Calm down and speak slowly so I c-c-can understand you," Soko added in jest.

"Stop teasing him!" Catia snapped.

"The same can be said to you," Tusk mumbled from the back.

"What does he mean, Rinn? Have I been teasing you?" She tugged on his shirt with an innocent gleam in her eye.

"Don't worry about that, sweetheart," Rinn patted her on the head.

"Okay!" she responded giddily. She turned then scowled at Tusk and stuck out her tongue.

"Wow," mumbled Tusk.

"Let's just have some damn peace and quiet, ya bunch of blithering nancies," Soko snapped, and the other three started to snicker under their breath. "What's funny?" At this, the others started to cackle. "What's so damn funny, ya dafty dingwads?"

"It-it's the w-way you talk!" Rinn sputtered out in a fit of laughter.

"That's not even right. You can't do a man this way, it's just unethical." Soko cracked the reins and threw the horses into a gallop, throwing everyone into a fit to hang on. "Bunch of dirty bastards, I'll show you a thing or two," he grumbled as Rinn began to go over the side.

"Soko, wait! Just slow down now, this isn't fun," Rinn said in a panic as he went over the side and Tusk grabbed him by the collar, but the two of them went over the side, tumbling under the wagon with a thud.

"Gah, you crazy bastard! Stop the wagon!" Catia snapped as she slapped Soko in the face, and he pulled the horses to a stop. Once they were stopped, she jumped off the wagon and ran over to Rinn. "Are you okay? Did you get run over by that barbarian?" Catia queried as she checked him all over, and Rinn stood and dusted himself off.

"I'm fine, Tusk, are you all right?" Rinn removed his cloak and shook the dirt out of it and put it back on.

"Yeah, I'm all right. I don't understand how, but I am." Tusk got down on all fours and shook off, causing everyone to pause in their tracks. "What?"

"Nothing," Rinn replied, looking at the ground with an impish grin.

"Well, come on now, we need to keep moving," Soko barked from the wagon.

"You just hold on one minute, you barbaric asshole!" Catia snapped and flew at him in a fit of rage. "You damn near killed him, you shithead! What were you thinking, huh? Answer me!"

"Well—"

"Don't you try and talk your way out of this!" Catia snapped. She rolled up her sleeve and punched Soko in the jaw, knocking him cold.

"Damn, what a right hook she's got!" Tusk said in shock.

"You have no idea." Rinn shook his head and dragged Soko to the back of the wagon then flopped him in. As he hopped back on the front, he found Catia sitting there with the reins in hand.

"Can you teach me how to drive so I can be useful to you?" She looked at him with her big green eyes and pouted.

"Click your tongue twice and shake the reigns a little," he instructed with false professionalism.

Catia followed his instructions, and the horses started walking. Catia's eyes lit up with joy, and she cracked the reins harder, and the horses started to trot. "I'm doing it! I'm driving a wagon!"

Catia's smile lit up Rinn's world like the suns. Rinn smiled and kissed her on the cheek. "Keep it up, and I might teach you how to use a bow," he offered.

"Really? I would really love that!" She giggled and Rinn looked around the lands and watched as the second sun continued rising over the northern horizon, and a blue haze came over the land. "I love the second sun. The heat is sweltering, but it still reminds me of you," Catia added amiably.

"I think the gods should've just given us one sun, two is one too many." Rinn shed his cloak and tossed it in the back. Glancing to the side, he noticed Catia was pouting at him. "What?" he asked.

"You can't agree with me at all, can you?" She frowned.

"Not on this matter. It gets so hot." Rinn pulled out his sword and watched it change into the same blue haze as the second sun and Catia's eyes grew wide with amazement.

"It changed colors! How'd it do that?" She inquired, full of excitement.

"It's made from Solinius ore. It must be blessed by the gods or something," he replied as he studied it closely.

"Ooh, that's neat." She stuck her finger against the edge, cutting her finger. "It's too sharp," she added as she stuck her finger in her mouth.

"Why'd you touch the sharp part?" Rinn ripped off a piece of his shirt and wrapped it around her finger. "That should do it," he added as he held her hand gently and smiled.

"Thank you," she lifted her finger and sniffed the makeshift bandage "It smells like you."

"It is my shirt," Rinn said blatantly as he patted her on the head. He turned away and smelled the air. *I smell smoke,* he thought to himself. "Catia, I need the reins," he added with desperation in his voice.

"But—"

"Now! There's something wrong," he snipped. Catia handed the reins over to him and held onto his arm as he cracked them, drawing the horses into a gallop. *Where's that smell coming from? Is it the town or a forest fire?* he thought to himself as he drove the wagon up a nearby hill with a tall tree. "I'm gonna climb up you stay in the wagon," Rinn rushed up to the top of the tree with amazing agility and saw a huge plume of smoke rising up in the horizon in the direction they were headed. *What's going on?* he thought to himself. He jumped down from the top of the tree, landing back in the seat of the wagon and cracked the reigns. *"Ha-ya!"*

"What's going on?" Catia asked.

"Someone's burning the town we were supposed to shack up in tonight." Rinn glared ahead with rage in his eyes. *It must be the empire. I just don't know how they knew, or if it was just something done for the sake of doing it,* he thought to himself. "We'll have to stay out of the towns if we want to avoid getting into any trouble," Rinn added as he pulled back on the road.

"What's all that smoke?" Tusk asked, rubbing his eyes. "Is something on fire?" Tusk's eyes grew wide with fear, and his ears twitched "There are people screaming. I can hear them. Rinn, what's happening?"

"It's as I feared. Someone knows about what's been going on. I knew I felt something off since a while ago, like I was being watched," Rinn replied as he looked in the back of the wagon and saw Soko was still unconscious. "Wake him, we need to get off the road and start setting up a camp here pretty soon."

Tusk held some mead under Soko's nose, and he jerked awake.

"Jeez, your sweetie's a mean one," he said, rubbing his jaw.

"Now's not the time. Someone is burning the town up ahead. Can you tell us what's going on using some of that dark magic?" Rinn cracked the reins, and Soko vanished before their eyes.

"Should we stop and wait for him to get back?" Tusk looked at Rinn, and he pulled off the road and into the patch of trees.

"Rinn, what's going on?" Catia tugged on Rinn's sleeve, and he held her hand, rubbing it with his thumb.

"We're being watched by someone or something, and it's been telling the empire where we've been heading, and they cut us off. Well, that's the theory at least." Rinn hopped off the wagon and pulled a sack out of the back. "We'll make camp-camp here."

"Camp-camp?" Tusk said, trying not to laugh. "Who calls it camp-camp?"

"Forget I said it. Quinn almost brainwashed me with his weirdness," Rinn added, shaking his head.

"Why do we have to make camp so early in the day?" Catia asked with worry and panic all over her face from Rinn's words.

"It's to keep from having to collect wood after dark. This way we can stay by the fire all night without having to risk being bitten by a snake or something worse," he replied as he turned to her. Rinn held her hands and looked her in the eyes "There's nothing to worry about okay. I'm not gonna let anything happen to you." Suddenly, Soko reappeared in front of them with his eyes hollowed and covered in blood and soot.

"They burned it all looking for us. I killed a few and left them hanging. We have until morning. No fires tonight." Soko sat down in the dirt and clenched his fists. "How did they know about us?"

"I don't know, but I had a bad feeling that they would." Rinn looked around at his companions and saw fear in their eyes. "We need to figure out a plan," he added, attempting to ease their minds.

"There's one problem with that. If they knew about us, that means they knew about Theon and that means they're in danger," Soko added.

"We have to go save them! Father, Millie, and Bjorn!" Catia started to run for the road, but Rinn stepped in front of her and wrapped his arms around her. "Let go of me! They need us!" She pounded Rinn's chest and started to cry hysterically.

"I'm sure my three best students are more than enough to handle what troops they had. They'll also know not to let the messengers get away," Soko explained as he placed a hand on her head, and she stopped crying and looked up at him.

"You mean my father can fight? You taught him?" Catia asked as she clenched Rinn's shirt in her fists.

"Your pappy could kill hundreds if not thousands back in the day. I'm absolutely sure that those two can keep everyone safe. Quinn might lose his mind though." He smiled and turned to Tusk "We're gonna need those ears on watch tonight," he added, glancing at Fang.

"Understood," Tusk whistled, and his crimloch hopped out of the wagon with Cadius in tow. "Fang, climb that tree, and if you see anyone other than us, call for help."

The creature nuzzled his face and went straight up the tree.

"That's just plain weird," Soko added, shaking his head. "Talks to feckin' animals."

"At least I don't just vanish and reappear!" Tusk snapped.

"He's got a point," Rinn added as he poured out a sack of rocks.

"I'm simply bending the temporal void between life and death," Soko said plainly.

"That's not simple at all!" Rinn and Tusk responded in unison.

"Maybe not to you two, but to me it's pretty normal." Soko pulled out a bag of food and set it out then followed up with a barrel of mead. *"Young lady!"* Soko boomed, causing Catia to drop Cadius and sending Rinn into a panic, causing him to fall on his face.

"Y-yes?" she asked, terrified of Soko's glowing coals.

"Be a dear and help your boyfriend check our perimeter," he replied gently with a smile.

"O-okay." She stood, and Rinn took her by the hand, and they headed off into the woods. They went on for about thirty paces when Rinn stopped and looked at her. "What is it, Rinn? Are you mad at me for coming along?" She queried, looking down at the ground. "I know I have to be the cause of all this trouble. I've always brought bad luck."

"Stop going on about that this instant!" Rinn snapped. "I couldn't begin to describe how happy it makes me to know you're safe," he added, but she kept looking down at the ground and started to cry. "Catia, I know it's tough, but you have to be strong. You don't need to be worried unless Soko is. He knows that they're gonna be okay." He wiped the tears off his cheeks and ran his fingers through her hair.

"I guess you're right, I should be stronger. And I will be!" She forced a smile, and the two of them started walking around the camp. Rinn stopped and took a knee by a set of tracks he noticed.

"Oh shit," Rinn said as his eyes grew wide with fear.

"What's wrong?" Catia asked as she stooped over in front of him. He looked up, and he noticed he could see her breasts through her blouse, then she looked down. "You looked!" She threw sticks at him, and Rinn tried catching them to no avail.

"It wasn't on purpose! I swear, love, I didn't do it on pur—" He was cut off when her next missile glanced off his mouth. "Catia please calm down." Rinn looked up, and his eyes grew wide with fear as he realized he'd just said the one thing he shouldn't have.

"Calm...down?" She dove on top of him, and a flurry of attacks followed suit, and Rinn managed to kiss her before she melted into him. "You big dummy," she said through her lips as she kissed him deeply. "You're not supposed to do a girl like this, this isn't—" Rinn cut her off with another kiss, and they held each other tightly. Catia smiled as she pressed herself against him. "Damn it! I can't stay mad at you. I love you, Rinn." She nuzzled against his chest.

"I love you too, Catia. Can we focus on the problem at hand now?" Rinn smiled, and she looked at the ground.

"What made those tracks?" she asked, looking at him with fear in her eyes.

"Hell birds," Rinn responded with eyes of ice.

"Are those the creatures that killed ten of your men?" Catia queried in panic.

"Yeah. Mean-ass things. They're just a bit smaller than a horse and are pack hunters. This track is fresh too. It was probably a scout, and it's likely already gone for the rest of the pack," Rinn explained with a worried look.

"I've never seen you nervous before. Is everything gonna be all right?" Catia queried, looking around nervously.

"Yeah, it should be fine. It'll be a drag, but I might not die." Rinn sighed, looking into the trees.

"How many are in the pack?" Tusk queried as he walked up behind them.

"Could be ten or forty," Rinn responded as he headed back to the camp.

"That's bad. I don't know what forty is, but it sounds like a lot." Tusk sighed, rubbing his face. "Well, let's go tell creepy guy we need to get ready for a fight," he added as he walked back to camp.

"C'mon, Catia! It's dangerous to be alone right now," Rinn said as he entered the clearing.

"What is it?" Soko asked, looking to Rinn through his bushy brows.

"Hell birds. The scout already came and left. He'll bring the pack back with him," Rinn explained.

"Shite, that's not good. I hate the damn things. The whole time yer huntin' them, they be huntin' you too," Soko replied, lowering his head. "Hell birds on the first day—great!" he added with a sigh.

"What should I do?" Catia queried, holding a thick seasoned branch.

"Just stay in the wagon and protect Cadius," Rinn replied as he drew his sword and sat down at the base of a tree facing into the clearing.

"Okay," Catia said as she scooped up Cadius and put him in the wagon.

"They'll be here at sunset. That's when they like to hunt," Tusk said as he scaled a tree on the other side of the clearing.

"Sooner. They'll hit us with full force in about twenty minutes," Rinn responded as he rolled his shoulders. They waited in silence for a few moments when hurried footsteps started coming into earshot. The footsteps danced around the camp for a few minutes—then all was silent. Suddenly, a hair-raising screech broke the silence, and one of the creatures jumped out of the trees. The arms and neck bore more feathers than scales while the legs had only colorful scales. Wielding huge talons on its feet and hands, along with razor-sharp teeth, this creature was truly terrifying. It screamed, sending a chill down Rinn's spine. Without a sound, Rinn sprang into action and killed the beast where it stood in a single blow. Another ambushed him from the brush, knocking him on his back. He struggled to keep the beast's fangs at bay when Tusk leaped out of the tree and stuck an ax in its skull, killing it instantly.

"Thanks," Rinn said as he gracefully flipped back to his feet and secured his footing.

"Don't mention it," Tusk replied as he posted up back-to-back with Rinn. The two of them held their ground against beast after beast, slaying each one with a single swift strike until the pack finally paused the assault. Suddenly, as if out of thin air, the alpha of the pack walked into the clearing and began circling the two of them. It was a large male with scars on his face and neck. He circled the two of them, inspecting their every move. He looked at his fallen pack members and snorted then, letting out three earsplitting barks. Then, as if he had weighed the risk of continuing the assault, the creature retreated into the woods, and the sounds of his pack following him swiftly made their way back the way they came.

"Get a fucking fire started now!" Rinn shouted out.

"Already on it," Soko replied as he held a piece of wood, and it burst into flames.

"How did you do that?" Rinn asked in shock.

"Black magic," Soko replied sarcastically as he shook his hands and rolled his eyes, tossing more wood on the fire.

"Now I can't tell if you're being serious," Rinn shook his head and left him to tend the fire. *I should be able to do stuff like that too, right?* he thought to himself as he went on into the trees and gathered up another bundle of wood and set it on the pile. "Can you teach me how to use magic?"

"That just depends on if you have magic to begin with, laddie," Soko replied as he looked up to Rinn and smiled. "Let's find out together if you do have magic," he added, raising a finger.

"How do we find ou—?" Rinn was interrupted when Soko blasted him with a small blast of fire, blowing him clear across the camp, sending Catia into a panic.

"Rinn! Are you okay?" She rushed over to his side and shook him, but he didn't respond. Then she flew at Soko with a big stick, beating him in the head and ribs. Meanwhile, Rinn stood up and dusted himself off with an impish grin while Tusk rolled around in the dirt laughing.

"I'm okay. It was mostly just the fall that hurt." He walked over to Catia, who was still beating Soko, and took her stick away. "I can't have my new magic teacher beat to death," he added impishly.

"She doesn't hit nearly hard enough, but I can say your little girlfriend has a lot of mana emanating from her, especially when she gets mad. Not that she knows any prayers for ice magic," Soko explained as he dusted himself off and gave Rinn an impish smirk. "You didn't die so you can use magic," he added, blatantly gesturing at Rinn.

"So if I *couldn't* use magic, you would've killed me!" Rinn scowled at Soko as he chuckled.

"Well, it's not like that. Much would've been enough to do any physical damage. It would've only stopped your heart for a bit it all," Soko replied casually.

"That's still so dangerous," Rinn mumbled under his breath.

"That's the power of magic, boy. You have to understand that wielding this level of power requires a great amount of responsibility, because ultimately, it means you hold the power to choose who lives and who dies," Soko added as his eyes hollowed under his brow.

"I see." Rinn sighed. "I don't think I want to have this type of power just yet. I don't feel like I could control it enough," he added, looking at his hands.

"Have you ever meditated, laddie?" Soko queried.

"No. Quinn said I only needed to work on sword skills and the like," Rinn replied casually.

"Well, I should've expected that from Quinn. Sit, I'll teach you the basics for now," Soko replied. He walked into a different section of trees and gestured at a large patch of moss for them to sit on. Rinn took off his sword and sprawled out on the moss, then he looked over to Soko to see that he was giving him an ill look. "Sit on your arse and fold yer legs in, ya shithead," he snapped.

"All right," Rinn replied as he followed the instructions.

"Straighten your back like this," Soko sat down and got into position and showed him how he should be seated. Rinn mirrored him and Soko nodded. "Now, close your eyes," he added.

"Okay," Rinn closed his eyes and waited.

"Now look inside yourself. What do you see?" Soko queried.

"I see...a swirling ocean with seven whirlpools," Rinn replied sarcastically.

"Well, you shouldn't see anything, you have your eyes closed," Soko responded in kind.

"Well, I can see colors in the darkness," Rinn added.

"Good, focus on those colors. Think of them as a fire and use your breath to fuel them," Soko replied.

"All right, I'll try." Rinn focused on the swirling lights and took long, deep breaths, then he noticed they were growing brighter and brighter with each breath. He continued his efforts when suddenly it felt as if he was being slowly dipped into a warm pool of water. The warmth rushed over him completely, and he felt like his body was light as a feather.

Soko sat and watched in astonishment as Rinn's entire body began to glow. *This kid is amazing! Not only did he catch on to it quickly, but he's already got enough power to make himself glow. If he can master this as quick as he learns it, he would be nearly unstoppable,* he thought to himself. Suddenly, the patch of moss they were sitting on began to grow bigger. *The plants are reacting to him!* He looked at Rinn with bewilderment. "Rinn, you're amazing, you know that?"

"Hmmm?" Rinn queried as he opened his eyes, causing the glow to disappear. "Wasn't the moss smaller before?" he inquired as he looked around.

"You're almost completely hopeless," Soko replied blatantly.

"Awww, I thought I was doing good," Rinn added, hanging his head.

"Guys, something is coming," Tusk said calmly as he readied his ax. Simultaneously, Cadius and Fang readied themselves for battle as Rinn drew his sword.

"Catia, get in the wagon and don't make a sound until I come get you," Soko said sternly.

"Do as he says," Rinn whispered. Catia hurried over to the wagon and climbed inside, hiding under the tarp. "Tusk, what's coming?"

"Demons, I'd say at least fifteen. I've never heard of them traveling in anything more than pairs this far north," Tusk added as his voice started to shake.

"Damn it all! They see the smoke!" Soko cursed himself, and a dark aura surrounded him. Suddenly, his eyes lit aflame along with his arms. "Bring it! C'mon!" As he spoke, ten soldiers in imperial armor broke through the trees. Their eyes were crimson, and they had black onyx horns growing from their foreheads.

"Soko the Soulless! You are to be taken into custody under the order of his majesty, Dominic Shoindal II, under the act of treason and harboring a fugitive Drumaulian! What say you to these charges?" The leader of the troops pointed his sword at them.

"I say you can all go and beg my master Aesirith for forgiveness for all I care! Burn in hell, you damn dirty heathens!" Soko unleashed a powerful flame and engulfed the guards, burning them to ash. "Who's next!? I've been dying to satisfy my goddess's taste of death!"

Meanwhile, Tusk and Rinn had terrified looks on their faces as Soko licked his lips in anticipation as if he were expecting some form of delicious meal.

"Are we sure he's not a demon?" Tusk asked, pointing his finger.

"*Him?* A demon? Oh no, no, no, no. Do you want to see the power of a royal-blooded demon?" An eerily calm voice rang out as a lone man walked into the camp. "Please allow me to introduce myself. I am Dominic Shoindal III, the firstborn son of the emperor and sole heir to the throne. You have all sullied the name of my empire, and the only option for you is to die," he added as he drew his sword with a bow. And the air suddenly grew dense, making it hard to breathe.

"Soko, do the fire thing!" Rinn shouted, but Soko was frozen in fear. *Damn, it's no good, he's petrified,* Rinn thought to himself as he focused his power. As time slowed, he charged at the demon prince and sliced his arm clean off, but the prince only cracked a twisted smile.

"Not bad," Dominic replied with an indifferent expression. Then Dominic snatched up Rinn and held him up by his throat. "You cut my arm off, you damn filthy worm! I'll kill you, and I will indeed kill you slowly." Suddenly, Soko appeared and grabbed Dominic, transporting the three of them away.

Rinn heard only what could be described as a thousand screams all at once, and then only the deafening sound of wind in his ears. He opened his eyes only to realize Soko had transported them high enough in the sky that he could see above all the mountains and even the southern sea. Panicked, he searched for Soko to discover he was being held hostage by Dominic. He thrusted over and sliced Dominic down the back, causing him to let go of Soko, then he instantly vanished.

Rinn looked at Prince Dominic and shouted, "Well, isn't this a wonderful view? It could be a view to die for!"

"I won't be killed by such a measly attempt as this, foolish boy!" Dominic lunged toward Rinn, and Soko appeared behind Rinn, then the two of them vanished. *"Damn you!"* he cursed as he continued to plummet toward the ground.

The next thing Rinn knew, he fell back into the camp and found Tusk fighting the remaining four demon guards with an ax in each hand, but he could only focus on defending himself. Then he noticed the prince's arm crawling across the ground toward the wagon. *It's after her!* Rinn thought to himself as he staggered to his feet. "Tusk! Hurry it up on killing those four!" he rushed over to the wagon and snatched the arm and tossed it into the fire, causing it to erupt into flames and turn to ash. He pulled the wagon cover back and was greeted by a club to the side of his head, leaving him unconscious on the ground. Meanwhile, Soko was hanging the remaining guards in the trees.

"Tusk! Get Rinn back into the wagon! We're heading for the mountains!" Soko ordered. Tusk rushed through the camp and threw Rinn in the back like he was some form of luggage, then he gathered the supplies while Soko doused water on the fire to put it out. Then he ripped a huge pine limb off a nearby tree.

"What's that for?" Tusk asked as he helped Cadius and Fang into the wagon.

"It's to cover our tracks, halfwit," Soko pulled a rope out of the back of the wagon and tied the branch to the back needles down. Meanwhile, Catia was crying hysterically.

"I killed him! Oh gods, I've killed my love!" She threw herself over Rinn's seemingly lifeless body, and he opened his eyes then gave a mischievous grin. Suddenly, Catia kissed him deeply, and he turned as red as her hair.

"Urm, alurve shweetnesh," he said through her lips. She pulled away in shock, and he wiped the tears away from her eyes as blood poured down the side of his face from the gaping wound she'd given him. "You should know that I wouldn't die so easily," he added as she ripped her dress and tended to his wound, and he winced.

"Don't be such a baby," she snapped with her voice shaking as much as her hands. Tears welled up in her eyes, and Rinn smiled at her then held her hands in his.

"Do you want to go home?" He closed his eyes and smiled at her.

"What gave you the idea I'd ever want to leave you?" She pulled her hands away and grabbed a stone cup and threw it to Tusk. "Fill this up with mead." He filled it and reached it back to her, then she dashed it on the wound, causing Rinn to writhe in pain.

"It burns! It burns!" He tried to hold his head but found he couldn't stand to touch it, causing Catia to giggle.

"You're such a baby. It's not even that bad." She finished cleaning the wound, much to Rinn's dismay. "At least you have a beautiful girl like me caring for you," she added pretentiously.

"I guess you're right," Rinn replied with a light chuckle. *Well, at least she's back to normal,* he thought to himself. Suddenly, Rinn had an epiphany, and a look of fear came into his eyes. "The palace! Soko, can you go take a look?"

"Already did. Everything is fine there, and they know we're okay. And they know basically what happened and are ready for any unwanted visitors," Soko replied as he cracked the reins and brought the horses to a trot, and they started back on the road. The second sun started to set on the southern horizon, and dusk fell over the land, giving everything a blue hue.

"The sunset is so beautiful," Catia said as she bandaged Rinn's head.

"Yes, it's almost as beautiful as you are," Rinn added amiably. He gazed upon the setting sun and admired the deep purple of the sky as Catia held him in her lap.

*****

Meanwhile, back at Theon's palace, the situation had changed drastically. A man in imperial armor leading eight men approached the gates. When he reached them, he noticed they were slightly open. He readied his gladius and motioned for his men to follow suit. He opened the gate cautiously and jumped through, only to find Juno watering the flowers.

"How can I be of service, mister soldier?" Juno queried amiably with a bright smile.

"Take me to the lord of this palace!" the man demanded, pointing his sword at her.

"But Lord Theon is conducting business with some other lords right now," Juno explained timidly.

"I am Commander Batius of the Satrisia Empire, and you will heed my command! It is his business with them I have business with, you little shit!" he snapped harshly, causing Juno to start crying.

"What's the meaning of this?" Theon snapped as he rushed through the courtyard with his broadsword in hand. It was large but not so large that it couldn't be used one-handed, and it had an extravagant pommel.

"You are under suspicion of treason against the crown! One with such charges should be mindful of their actions," Batius replied, pretentiously pointing his sword at Juno's throat.

"I don't recall swearing allegiance to any king or emperor! I was promised freedom so long as I stayed in my own lands!" Theon snapped as he took his stance.

"Make another move, and I'll kill this girl, traitor!" Batius responded as he pressed the blade against her throat. Juno's emerald eyes were filled with tears and terror, yet she did not make a sound.

"Juno, don't move, little sweetie. Everything will be all right," Theon cooed as he slowed his breath. "Solinius, grant my blade the light that guides the way. May the blessed rays of your children bring warmth to all who stand below them!" Theon said as his sword began to glow a silvery blue, and he shifted, holding the sword behind him. "Blessed rays after the storm," he added as he swung his sword with perfect form in the direction of the intruders, then he exited his stance.

"Why swing from ten feet away, you fool?" Batius queried as his men fell to the ground behind him. "What?" he added as he turned to discover they were all headless. He looked back to Theon in confusion then fell to his knees—and his head rolled off his shoulders with the same confused look on his face.

"It always confuses the last one," Theon said as he laid his sword down on his patio.

"Thank you, Lord Theon!" Juno sobbed hysterically as she buried her head into Theon's chest. "Shfank you sho mush!" she added looking up to him, revealing she'd left a rope of snot attached to his robe.

"It's quite all right, little one. I shall see you paid tenfold this fall for having to be in such dire straits," Theon replied, patting her head. "Let us go and tell everyone what's happened, and what is likely to come searching for their missing comrades," he added as the two of them rushed across the courtyard and into the palace. "Mille, Quinn! I've killed some more of the empire's troops! Could you clean them up for me?" he queried, shouting upstairs.

"We're busy!" the two of them shouted back in unison.

"Not pursuing that any further," Theon said as he turned and made his way back outside to the courtyard. As he rushed through the palace, he bumped into Kaya, knocking her to the floor.

"Hey, watch where you're going!" she snapped as she picked herself up and dusted off her uniform.

"Sorry, Kaya. I'm just out of sorts at the moment," Theon replied as he made his way out the door. He rushed across the courtyard to where the slain imperial soldiers lay and took a knee. "I pray to the great god Itrius, creator of all living beings. Forgive me, for I have slain a part of your creation. Grant them passage to judgment by your sister Aesirith, mistress of the dead. From dust we were created and to dust shall we return, amen," he added touching the dirt then his forehead as he rose to his feet. With this, the heads and bodies began to glow, then they vanished without a trace.

"That's the same spell you cast for Lady Astrid, isn't it?" Millie queried from behind as she put her hair up.

"Yeah, that was the most painful thing I ever had to do. I was forced to kill the woman I love," Theon said, falling to his knees.

"That's not what happened that day, and you know it! She was killed and turned into a ghoul by a demon," Millie snapped harshly.

"I know, I just can't help but feel like if I'd been with her, she would still be here," Theon responded with tears streaming down his face.

"Hindsight is as clear as a midsummer day, foresight is as foggy as a winter night," Quinn butted in as he walked into the courtyard.

"Don't use Soko's proverbs on me right now please. I never understand them," Theon replied as he flopped on his back.

"It means stop thinking about the past and start moving forward," Millie said as she sat down next to Theon.

"We've all been close since we were kids. You think my sister's kid is gonna get along with Rinn?" Quinn queried blatantly, looking up to the sky.

"Tusk is your nephew!?" Theon and Millie asked in shock.

"He smells just like her," Quinn replied, plainly glancing at them. "You think they're doin' all right out there?" he added, looking up to the sky.

"It's gonna be dark soon, so I assume they're making camp," Millie sighed as she laid down.

"Camp-camp." Quinn puffed as he sniffed the air. Suddenly, a grin creeped across his face, and he began chuckling under his breath. "The rest of them are coming. Heh-ha-ha. *Ahahahaha!*" He cackled as he drew his sword. It was the same make as Rinn's, but it had a slightly different tip, clearly made for slashing instead of piercing through armor. "These guys are mine!" he screamed as he rushed out of the gate.

"Just wait for them here! I'd like to see how little you've improved," Millie called out with a condescending look.

"I'll show you just how far ahead I've gotten! I finally surpassed you, love! Just kick back and enjoy the show," Quinn replied as he took his stance. He remained completely still and closed his eyes. The sound of soldiers marching came into earshot, and he cracked a smile. He took a deep breath and shifted his feet. The sound of rock grinding under his boots echoed off the palace walls as he solidified his stance. The soldiers marched up the hill and stopped a few paces in front of the gate. A soldier carrying the imperial flag stepped forward and cleared his throat.

"An envoy was sent to collect Lord Theon Helmfast for questioning, and they haven't returned, so we are here to enforce the emperor's word," the soldier explained, holding out a scroll.

"I can't read," Quinn replied with his eyes closed.

"Can you bring us to someone who can?" the soldier inquired with a smug look.

"I don't answer questions," Quinn replied as he shifted his stance. "Ten of you are having trouble breathing, the other twenty are sweating profusely. The one in the front smells nervous," he added as he looked down.

"Enough of this farce! I order you to—" the soldier bearing the flag was cut off by Quinn's blade. His throat was slashed open before he could even react, and he fell to the ground, choking on his own blood.

"These criminals are in possession of Solinius weapons! Arrest them!" one of the soldiers ordered. They charged Quinn all at once, but he gracefully dodged all their attacks without opening his eyes. He delivered three blows in an instant, killing three more of the soldiers.

"That's four," Theon said calmly as he sat up. A soldier came at Quinn from behind, but he glanced the attack off his sword and stabbed him in the gut. Without skipping a beat, he turned and slashed another through the chest, killing him swiftly. Four soldiers came at him, and he dropped to his knees, causing them to hit one another. He spun, slashing them all in one fluid strike, and delivered a fatal blow to each of them. He then killed a fifth that started heading toward Millie and Theon.

"I'm your opponent," Quinn said calmly. "Ten of you are dead, surely someone among you can bring me down," he added as he sheathed his sword and bladed himself toward his opponents. The remaining soldiers began to hesitate then suddenly rushed him all at once, but Quinn drew his sword, decapitating two of them in an instant, causing the remaining eight to step back. "Wise decision," he added with a disappointed look.

"He's better than me now," Millie puffed in frustration. "Just because—"

"You're a monster!" one of the soldiers said in rage.

"This coming from the soldiers who've raped and pillaged their way through this kingdom!" Quinn retorted, opening his eyes with a hateful look.

"You have no room to talk. I can tell that you've killed many men with that sword," one of the soldiers in the back called out.

"There are certain rules to war, you know! The gods say never to harm an innocent being or take up arms without a just reason. And if war is inevitable, you must not harm the landscape nor women and children. For if women and children take up arms against you, your cause is unjust, and you must be sent to Aesirith for judgment," Quinn replied sternly.

"Damn the gods! You mortal races are weak, so the least we can do is put some real strength in your gene pool!" the soldier retorted.

"Would you just shut up! I don't rape! I got a wife and kids back home in the capital. I don't wanna die here!" one of the other soldiers called out.

"Cowardice is forbidden!" three of the soldiers called out as they ran the terrified soldier through, leaving him crumpled on the ground. Quinn took this opportunity to slay the three then turned to face the remaining four.

"Would anyone else like to bow out?" Quinn queried with a cold look. The soldiers looked at one another and steeled themselves for a fight to the death. "I see, that's too bad," he added as he retook his stance. The remaining four rushed him together, and Quinn disappeared from their sight, causing them to stop and put their guard up. They stood in a tightly formed circle, each taking their best respected forms. With agility as silent as a butterfly's wingbeat, Quinn dropped into the center of them. With a single swing of his sword, he ended their lives before they even knew he was there. "Now for the one that's still kicking," he added as he started pulling the swords out of the soldier who was run through by his own comrades.

"I'm pretty sure he's dead, love," Millie called out with a confused look.

"Like I've said, these evil shits don't die unless you use Solinius steel," Quinn snipped.

"What're you plotting?" Theon queried, raising a brow.

"I found us some information," Quinn replied with a blank expression as he watched the soldier regenerate in a grotesque manner.

"Fucking hell!" the soldier called out as he regained consciousness.

"I have a question for you," Quinn said coldly, holding his blade to the soldier's throat.

"Ask it then," he responded hatefully.

"Can you draw an up-to-date map of the imperial capital?" Quinn inquired, raising a brow.

"No, I've never even seen it," the soldier replied.

"Second question, how many people have you eaten?" Quinn followed, bringing blood out of his neck.

"Dozens," the soldier responded with a twisted grin. Without a word, Quinn severed his head then flicked the blood off his blade. "I guess I was wrong," he added as he sheathed his sword.

"You know he was probably just saying what he was trained to say," Theon said with a disappointed look.

"Don't care. The eating-people one wasn't a lie like having a wife and kids was. I just thought he was the kind of coward who'd sell out his own to save his own skin," Quinn replied with a cold look.

"That look is why I fell in love with him. I mean, sure, I appreciate his soft side. But I sure do love it when a man is the best of both worlds," Millie said, biting her lip. "C'mon, Quinn, I'm on break for the rest of the day," she added, tugging on his sleeve.

"With pleasure, love," Quinn replied with a smile as the two of them walked back into the palace.

"You're just going to leave this mess in my courtyard?" Theon queried impatiently.

"Oh, all right, fine!" Millie snapped as she walked up and looked over to the dead soldiers. She snapped her fingers, and blue flames erupted from the corpses, leaving no trace of their existence. "Now I'm on break!" she snapped harshly as she dragged Quinn into the palace.

"At least tell everyone today is fieldwork! I don't want the children hearing you two making another!" Theon called out as the door closed. He waited a few moments in silence, and the rest of the staff walked out with hollow eyes. Their expressions were blank as they assembled in front of Theon.

"Let's go to the fields." They all sighed dryly.

"I have a new invention that's gonna make this quick and easy, kids, so don't worry," Theon responded as he led them out to the shed. "I just need two oxen, and I can cut all of a day's wheat in an hour!" he exclaimed as he swung open the doors and revealed a modified wagon with blades set up on either side of the wagon. "I hooked these blades up to a belt on a pulley system, and when the wagon moves forward. it spins the blades fast enough to cut wheat," he explained.

"Lord Theon's made another death machine," Kaya groaned.

"Lord Theon, sir, might I add that the last thing you made like this ended up ruining half an acre of wheat. It sent a blade flying into the forest, sir," Wesley said with a worried look.

"Not to worry, Wesley, I've perfected it. It's taken a few years, but I've finally perfected it. I call it the ox-powered wheat cutter," Theon responded with a confident look.

"You're absolutely sure it will work?" Wesley queried, looking over the new creation.

"Absolutely sure," Theon responded in assurance.

"Kaya, fetch the oxen. They like you since you raised them," Wesley said, glancing over to her.

"Okay," Kaya sighed doubtfully. She hurried over to the barn and opened the door. "Hoog, Goob! C'mon, boys, time for work," she called out. Without a problem, the two oxen unlatched their stalls with their horns and made their way out of the barn. Kaya waited on them at the door and greeted them with a hug. The oxen draped their heads over each of her shoulders in the embrace. Hoog was a slate blue, and Goob was dirt brown—both massive in size. She hopped on Goob's back and pointed to Theon. The oxen lumbered over and backed up to the wagon.

"Say what you want, but Kaya is the best animal trainer I've ever hired," Theon said with a smile.

"If they get hurt, I'll hurt you," Kaya snapped as she rushed over to the fields. Everyone watched in silence as Theon secured the harnesses and pulled the wagon out to the fields.

"By the gods, the thing works!" Wesley exclaimed as he watched Theon drive his invention across the first plot, cutting the wheat at the perfect length.

"Just follow behind me and pick it up, and we'll be done in half the time!" Theon called out. Without a word, the staff fell in and started gathering wheat.

"Theon may have just revolutionized farming," Wesley said with his eyes aglow. "Our Lord Theon is a mad genius!" he added with a chuckle.

CHAPTER 5

AN OLD FRIEND
AND A NEW ALLY

Meanwhile, Rinn and his friends traveled through the farm roads, only stopping to water the horses. He watched as the scenery changed from rolling fields of wheat to a scorched, barren wasteland. He looked ahead to see the smoldering remains of the village, but he noticed there was no smell of death in the air. "What happened to everyone?" he queried to himself as they made their way through the burned town. The scorched buildings and eerie silence made it clear that the Shoindal had killed everyone in the town. "I can't believe they did this just because we *might* have been here," Rinn muttered.

"There's nothing we can do about it, they've always been this way," Soko whispered.

"It's just awful." Catia buried her head into Rinn's chest and sobbed. "I wish we had something more than mercenaries to defend the people, I feel so useless." She clenched Rinn's shirt in her fists.

"It's not your fault, sweetheart. The empire is to blame, they're the ones who did this. Besides, we mercenaries take pride in fighting. I'm sure the ones who lived here went down fighting hard defending the townsfolk." Rinn stroked her hair, and Soko stopped the wagon. "Why are you stopping?"

"There's still quite a few souls who can't find peace. As an Aesiri, it's my duty to help them." He crouched down and sat on his knees while mumbling words nobody else could understand. Suddenly, Rinn heard ghostly wails, and then everything faded back to silence. "That should have them taken care of. Now they can go on to the next world," Soko added as he stood and gave a bow of respect.

"You act like a psycho, but you're pretty nice." Tusk patted him on the shoulder and smiled. "Teach me how to fight like you did the others," he added as he started pestering Soko with his ax handle.

"Sure. But we've other things to take care of first," Soko replied as he hopped back on the wagon. He cracked the reins and started on the main road to go out the other side of the town.

"Does it start with leaving me behind in a ghost town?" Tusk called out as he sprinted after them and clambered up into the wagon. The six of them made their way out of the town, traveling through the golden fields of wheat, watching them roll like waves in the wind.

"They would've had a plentiful crop this year. It's a shame that it'll all go to waste," Rinn said as he lowered his head.

"I'll see to it their hard work won't go to waste, and that any survivors who were outside the town get all the profits so they can rebuild." Catia clenched her fist and looked up to the sky.

"Sometimes you really do act like a proper lady," Rinn said impishly.

"*Sometimes?* I'll have you know I'm the only one here who has been taught proper etiquette and how to handle court affairs. Compared to me, you're all just a bunch of sword-swinging brutes." She folded her arms and turned away from them.

"I know. It's part of the reason why I'm so lucky to have you," Rinn laid his head on her lap, and she ran her fingers through his hair then clenched it in her fists.

"You'd be best to never forget it," she replied in a menacingly sweet voice.

"You're absolutely right, love," Rinn concurred as he winced in pain. She released her grip and continued to play with his hair. Cadius waddled over and pounced on Rinn, and he wrestled with the pup with his hand. Venturing through the open road, they watched as the scenery changed from golden fields to grassy plains filled with hulking boulders. "We're getting closer to the mountain pass. It's a little more dangerous on account of beasts, but it will shorten the trip to a day instead of a month." He raised up and fidgeted around in the supplies then pulled out a huge piece of jerky.

"Can I have some?" Catia asked as her stomach growled. Rinn reached for the piece he'd gotten for himself, and she tried to take a bite but failed. "Could you maybe make it bite-sized for me?" She reached it back to him embarrassed, and he smiled as he tore her off a bite then fed it to her.

"Can you guys get any more sickening?" snapped Tusk as he climbed out of the back and into the passenger seat of the wagon.

"We can be, yes," Rinn said sarcastically. He ripped off another piece and gave it to Catia, and she nibbled on it as neat as she could. He looked and saw that Fang and Cadius were looking at the meat like a child would sweets. "Fine, you can have some." Rinn reached into the bag and pulled out one hulking piece of smoked beef and a good thick piece of jerky and gave the biggest to Fang while Cadius got the smaller piece. The two of them gnawed on the hunks of meat until they only had bones—then Rinn felt the wagon shift.

"We've made it to the mountain pass, I think," Soko called out as he reached in the back and poured himself another glass of mead. Rinn moved up to the front and took the reins from Soko.

"I'll drive from here, but keep your wits about you. There's a reason why this is a last resort." Rinn brought the horses to a slow walk.

"Why is this a last resort?" Catia came out from the back and switched places with Tusk.

"There's a dangerous beast that's laid claim to this mountain." He readied his bow and gave Catia the reins.

"Why'd you give her the reins to my wagon?" Soko babbled out from inside his cup.

"Because you're already drunk," Rinn replied plainly as he scanned the area.

"What kind of beast is it anyway?" Tusk asked as he rummaged around in the back of the wagon.

"It's a banesimian. He's about fourteen feet tall," Rinn answered as he continued looking as they made their way up the mountain.

"A *banesimian*! Those are the worst beasts you can run into! They're powerhouses, and they don't fight fair! They drop down on top of you from the trees, and they *throw* trees and big rocks and all kinds of shit!" Tusk had a look of panic on his face as he scanned around searching for the creature. "How do you know it's even up here?"

"I ran into it when I was hunting deer." Rinn smiled and pulled up his shirt and pointed at three of his scars. "He gave me these, the only reason I'm alive is because I jumped in the river." He chuckled and noticed Catia was staring at him intensely.

"Why is this the first time I'm hearing of this?" She grabbed a fistful of his hair, and he started laughing.

"Because I didn't want you to worry about something that had already been fixed," he replied, still focusing on finding the beast. She let go of his hair, and they continued up the mountain. Rinn remained on guard as the scenery changed from thick forest to barren fields of rock as they approached the summit of the mountain. The rocks seemed to glow in the moonlight, and others seemed to have stars of their own inside them. Catia pulled the wagon off the road as they reached the summit, and they all got out of the wagon to stretch their legs. Rinn walked over to the edge of a cliff to look out into the world before him. He could see the valleys littered with small villages and smoke rising out of a few chimneys. "Soko, can you come here for a moment? I'd like to show you where we're going," he inquired.

"Aye, just a minute, laddie." Soko stretched himself out as he walked over to him and looked out into the valley. "That isn't even a town. There's only like seven houses," he added as he continued stretching.

"I said it was a *few towns over,* not a town." Rinn turned and started over to the wagon when suddenly a horrendously deep growl vibrated in his chest. Time slowed as he turned to see that a banesimian had climbed over the cliff and was coming after him. Soko vanished at the sound of the growl, so Rinn leaped back and got between it and Catia. It roared so loud that Rinn felt like his eardrums were going to burst. *I need everything I've got to kill this thing, or we're done for!* he thought to himself. Suddenly, he felt a tingling surge of power swell up inside of him. He gripped his sword and noticed small bolts of lightning started rolling down his blade. The beast pounded its chest so hard it made a sound like hammers beating logs. As time slowed once again, he leaped forward, swinging for its head, but he could only cut its face because his sword bounced off the beast's skull. He panicked, causing time to resume its pace, and the beast swatted him away, holding its face in pain. He landed on his shoulder and slid to his feet. He lunged forward, thrusting his sword into the beast's ribs.

Seizing the opportunity, Tusk buried both his axes into the beast's chest, causing it to cough blood into his face. It threw them both away and howled in a horrible pain-filled rage. "What now?" Tusk screamed.

"We have to stab it in the throat, or it will rage on for hours, kill us, and then die!" Rinn leaped toward it to keep its attention away from Catia, then Soko appeared on its back, but it threw him away before he could attack. Rinn thrusted at its throat and blood gushed out. The beast held its throat swinging wildly until it finally fell limp upon the ground. Rinn walked up and stabbed it in the eye to make sure it was dead.

"Is it dead?" Catia asked as she walked up behind him.

"Yeah, it's dead. I just hope this one was alone and doesn't have any friends." He walked over to the wagon, wincing in pain, and pulled a rope out of the back and tied it to its feet.

"What do you think you're doing?" Soko snapped. "We can't haul this thing! If it does have friends, I'd rather have them not find us dragging this dead body. Thank you, have a blessed day but no. Not this one, boyo." He snatched the rope from Rinn then rolled it up and tossed it in the wagon.

"Okay, that's understandable," Rinn replied as he climbed up the back and lifted Catia into the wagon. Tusk pulled his axes out of its chest, and he trotted over and hopped into the wagon. Soko cracked the reins, and they crossed the barren summit and made their way down into the valley with haste. As they were traveling down the other side of the mountain, Soko turned to Rinn and offered him the reins. "Sure," he replied. As he took the reins, a huge rock landed beside the wagon. Panicked, the horses started to gallop down the hill, shaking the wagon so hard Rinn felt it was going to flip over. As he got them under control, a huge log smacked the wagon, causing it to slide across the dirt road. Rinn cracked the reins so the wagon didn't get in front of the horses, and they barely managed to pull it back straight.

"What the hell is happening?" Tusk screamed.

"It's the friends of the one we killed! They ain't very happy with us!" Soko replied.

"That much is obvious!" Rinn shouted as another rock soared over the wagon, crashing through a nearby tree.

"Can't this thing go any faster?" Catia asked as she struggled to keep herself steady in the back of the wagon. Suddenly, two banesimians jumped out of the trees and started running like men behind the wagon but couldn't quite keep pace and cut the pursuit. The party finally made it to the base of the mountain, and the beasts stopped their pursuit. Rinn kept the pace up until they were close to the village, then he slowed down to rest the horses. "Thank the gods. I can't believe we made it through that without getting hurt." She sighed.

"I'm glad everyone is okay too." Rinn felt as if a heavyweight had been lifted from his shoulders as they approached the first house. They made their way by four more and came to a stop by the sixth. "Etarios the blacksmith, I've come to speak with you about something!" Suddenly, a tall, brutish young man with coal-black hair made his way out of the house.

"What's up? How can I help? Oh gods, it's you. What have I done to offend you, Frumhal? You spiteful god." He shook his hands at the sky but received no response. "It's always good to see you, Rinn!" He snatched him up and squeezed him, making his bones crack.

"Good to see you too, Etarios. Do you think you could come with me for a job that's worth lots of money?" Rinn strained out and patted him on the shoulder.

"I am in need of money. I haven't had any work in quite some time, but it's only because nothing I make breaks. Nobody around here needs anything, so yeah, I'll tag along. Who's it for?" He stroked his short beard and patted his leg.

"Lord Theon Helmfast," Rinn replied with a smirk.

"Lord Theon wants me to work for him?" he said in shock.

"Yes, but for now we'd like to rest for a little while." Rinn smiled and turned and saw the wagon. Everyone else was already gone. "Soko must've already took them home. Well, he'll be back in just a minute." Then Soko reappeared where the wagon had disappeared.

"C'mon then. Times a wastin'," Soko muttered as he walked over. Rinn placed a hand on Etarios's shoulder as he walked up and took them both by the arm, then screams filled their ears when suddenly they were standing in Theon's courtyard.

"What the hell just happened? How did we get here?" Etarios stood in shock, waiting for an answer.

"You get used to it," Rinn replied as he walked over to the wagon, and Catia sprang out of the back, wrapping herself around him.

"That was so much fun! Can we go on another adventure together?" she asked as she kissed Rinn's face all over and giggled.

"We almost died like five times. All in two days too! I don't see how it was fun." Rinn squeezed her gently, and she put her feet down, then they walked up to Theon.

"Sir Rinn! I hope your journey was a success." Theon opened his arms, and Catia greeted him with a hug. "My lovely daughter is growing up into a wonderful young lady."

"Speaking of that, the empire burned down the town we were supposed to stay in. I want some of our men to harvest the crops and distribute them to any survivors," Catia added as she looked up to her father, and he smiled down at her.

"I'll see to it that the crops don't go to waste, I promise." He placed his thick, callused hands on her shoulders. "Now that you're to be married, don't you think you should learn how to cook?"

"Aw, but I'm terrible at cooking. I always start fires in the kitchen." She twiddled her thumbs in embarrassment.

"Just listen to Millie and the other girls, and you'll be fine." Theon placed his hand on her cheek, rubbing it softly. "You know, if it weren't for Millie's mother, your mother would've been a terrible cook too."

"That's right, Lady Catia." Millie's soothing voice rang out over the courtyard. Her long brown hair flowed down to her waist, and Quinn was trotting behind her like a lost puppy. Quinn was naturally focused on the mountain range that laid upon Millie's chest. She rolled her eyes as she took Catia by the hand. "Come now, my lady, let us give these uncultured men our leave." She turned and pulled Catia into the palace.

"It's not my fault you have so much to look at, Millie, my dearest love!" Quinn called out.

"Quinn, you should be focused on something more than a woman's breasts," Theon said, shaking his head.

"Forgive me, My Lord, I just can't control myself around her." Quinn held his chest, and Soko slapped him in the back of the head.

"You're gonna end up with ten bastard children at this rate! Just tell her you love her and get it over with already," Soko snapped. "And we still have to give our new friend the details of what's going on." He pointed at Etarios, who was patiently waiting for an answer.

"Ah! The blacksmith Sir Rinn told me about. Come, I'm sure you're all quite ready for a good hard drink. I've a fresh batch of porter." They made their way into the palace, Cadius and Fang in tow. Theon turned and saw Fang was following them. "Is that a male crimloch?"

"Yeah. Why do you ask?" replied Tusk.

"I've had a female for a few years now. I was thinking we could breed them." Theon opened a door to an inner garden and revealed the crimloch to the rest of them, and Fang instantly ran to her side.

"It's fine with him, so it's fine with me." They made their way to the dining hall, and they all sat down together as Theon poured everyone a glass of porter.

"So, young blacksmith, what is your name?" Theon asked as he sat down.

"Etarios, your highness," he replied with a slight bow of respect.

"A fine name, I'll get straight to the point. I intend to start a rebellion against the empire and reclaim this land in the name of the gods. Will you forge the armor and weapons for my army?" Theon inquired as he took his seat.

"Without a doubt. I know what the empire really is." Etarios downed his glass, and a servant entered the room. "When do I get started?"

"As soon as you're rested and fed, you can go out to the forge I've had made for you," Theon replied.

"And the material?" Etarios queried.

"Solinius ore. It will defend our troops against the dark powers as well as our enemies' blades. Any man in normal armor would lose his mind when exposed to the dark energies, attacking anything, friend or foe. But with Solinius steel, we have the power of the sun god, Solstian, on our side. So, in turn, the magic that caused our defeat will be of little consequence." Theon raised his glass. "Cheers! To our good fortune!"

"Cheers!" everyone sounded off in unison.

"Sir Rinn, may I borrow you for a moment?" a young servant girl asked timidly.

"Yes, of course." He stood and followed the young girl into the hall. "Is there something you need help with?"

"Well, it's Lady Catia, she's being so hard on herself, and now she's locked herself away in her room. Could you go talk to her and see if you can calm her down?" The young girl's face turned crimson as she spoke.

"I'll try and figure out what she's having trouble with." He turned and headed up the stairs and found himself at Catia's bedroom door. A sudden feeling of anxiety overcame him as he knocked on the door.

"Come in, I'm only changi—" She was cut short when Rinn swung the door open, and she was caught half-naked.

"I'm so sorry!" Rinn slammed the door behind him without realizing he'd forgotten to leave first.

"What are you doing in here?" she asked in shock as she covered her porcelain-like skin with her bedsheets.

"One of the servant girls said you were being hard on yourself again, so I came to check on you. I wasn't trying to peep in on you while you were changing, I promise!" Rinn covered his face and prostrated himself on the floor.

"Oh, so you weren't trying to peep on your own fiancée, huh? Am I not worth peeping on?" She dropped her bedsheets and walked over to him with a mischievous smile.

"That's not what I said!" he replied in panic, keeping his eyes closed. *This is a trap laid by Millie and Catia both, I just know it. They sent that young girl so I wouldn't suspect them of anything. How could I fall for something so obvious?* he thought to himself. Rinn opened his eyes only to find Catia's milky white breasts in front of him followed by her angelic smile.

"They only say it's bad for you to see me in my wedding dress. They didn't say anything about this." She wrapped her arms around him and put his face between her breasts, causing his face to turn a shade of crimson. Rinn lost all will to fight her advance, and he went limp on the floor. She leaned over, kissing him deeply as he lay there helpless. "Don't you love me Rinn? Don't you want to take me here and now?"

"I still don't know if you know what that means," he said as he twitched on the floor.

"It's okay, Millie explained what love is to me in the kitchen just now, and I just can't wait anymore." She caressed him gently while he struggled to summon the willpower to resist. Suddenly, Tusk appeared and grabbed Rinn by the arm.

"I'm here to save you! Do not worry, my friend!" Tusk took off sprinting down the stairs as Catia cursed him for foiling her plot while Rinn was still dumbfounded by the sight of Catia naked.

"I'd given up on fighting her. Thank you, my friend. I thought I was done for. Theon would kill me if—"

"I'd kill you for what now?" Theon inquired as he walked up behind the two of them with an impish grin. He picked Rinn up by the hair. "Just what were you about to do to my daughter?"

"Nothing at all, Your Lordship!" He squirmed in pain as he struggled to his feet.

"Oh? You weren't trying to have your way with my daughter before marriage now, were you?" He tightened his grip, and it made a sound like leather grinding against itself.

"Of course not, My Lord. Such behavior would be unbefitting to a man of my title," Rinn strained out in pain.

"Very good." Theon released him, and he rubbed his head in pain. "I expect much from you, First Commander Rinn,"

"Oh dear, it seems my plan was ruined by the wildling." Millie giggled out as she walked by.

"It seems we've fallen prey to the scheming of women," Theon stated.

"So it does, sir!" Rinn and Tusk added in unison.

"Well, there's nothing we can do to compete with an enemy as formidable as this—but one thing." Theon's eyes gleamed with a gallant glimmer.

"What can we do, Lord Theon sir?" Rinn asked with his eyes gleaming with anticipation.

"We can party till the sun comes up!" Theon cast his cloak to the floor as they headed to the dining hall. "Men! We've scheming women around! Let us drink till we can no longer stand so we may avoid their devilish plots!" Theon exclaimed, clearly just wanting an excuse to drink.

"*Raaah!*" everyone cried out as they all drank their fill. They all laughed and made merry as the night went on.

"Hey, Wildling," Rinn slurred with his eyes glazed over.

"What's your problem?" Tusk slurred back with a foul expression.

"You're weak-looking," Rinn replied.

"Huh? What's that? You wanna fight?" Tusk queried hatefully.

"Damn right, you scrawny little bastard!" Rinn exclaimed as he stood up and poked Tusk's shoulder.

"Well, you've got one!" Tusk exclaimed as he tackled Rinn to the ground. The two of them fought like wild boars, knocking hunting trophies off the wall and causing a great commotion. They both had to withdraw after Rinn head-butted Tusk, and they both fell unconscious for a moment. Theon's laugh boomed through the palace along with the rest of them. They drank some more and told stories of old times together, then Rinn gave an extraordinary account of what had happened with the banesimian. This caused Theon to laugh until tears were rolling down his face, along with Quinn's. The seven of them held a mock wagon raid for the smoked beef and jerky, and this even brought the servants to roll in laughter as the men feasted on their so-called spoils of war. As the first sun rose, all was quiet around the palace. Rinn, being the only one awake, climbed up to the roof to watch the third moon set as the first sun rose. He looked out to the world before him knowing that after everything he and his friends had already been through, their journey had only just begun.

EPILOGUE

Meanwhile, far away from the celebrations, the demon prince was wandering aimlessly in the woods. "Damn those filthy mortals! I'll see to it they all pay for this insolence!" He looked up and sneered at the sun. "Cursed realm. If it weren't for the sunlight, my arm would've already grown back." He hobbled through the woods until he managed to find the road. "All right, which way is the imperial palace?" He looked either way up the road but couldn't tell where he was. "Damn this land to hell!" Dominic shouted as he made his way south, toward the heart of his empire. He hobbled onward until a lone horseman came galloping toward him.

"Your Highness! Where's the commander and his men?" The horseman queried as he dismounted.

"The rebels slew them," Dominic replied. "I need your horse. As you can see, I also suffered defeat at the hands of the lowly scum. Commoners no less," he snapped as he mounted the horse.

"Of course, sire, I shall do anything you desire," the horseman replied.

"If that's the case, how about you find that runaway bride of mine? I'd very much like to choke the life out of her for the embarrassment she put me through," Dominic ordered as he spurred the horse and galloped away.

"It will be done, sire," the horseman replied. "I shall post wanted posters sent to every nearby town ordering her to be returned alive!" he called out, and Dominic gave him a thumbs-up with a twisted grin.

"Give me your name soldier, so I know who to reward when my lovely bride returns!" Dominic called out as he halted the horse.

"My name is Allister, Your Highness!" he replied.

"Very well, Allister. If you should bring my new bride back to me unsullied, I shall reward you with the rank of commander," Dominic responded as he trotted a circle around Allister.

"Your will be done, My Liege," Allister replied with a bow.

"Naturally, I'm destined to rule the known world." Dominic spurred his horse and started galloping south once again. *I must tell father what's happening in the far reaches of the north. The rebels still live,* he thought to himself as he continued south. He rode until the scenery changed from rolling fields to deep, wide valleys. He kept riding until the capitol was finally in sight when the horse gave out from exhaustion. "Useless beast!" he said to himself. He kicked the dead horse and started for the capitol to warn his father of the coming storm.

ABOUT THE AUTHOR

Terrigan grew up in a small rural community in the Appalachian mountains. He enjoys going hiking in the mountains and off-roading. He also loves kayaking down the local rivers and watching animals in nature. He also enjoys spending time with his friends and family while he's not spending hours writing.

CPSIA information can be obtained
at www.ICGtesting.com
Printed in the USA
BVHW042338010623
665232BV00005B/134